THE
SILVER
COIN

MIKA MATHEWS

THE SILVER COIN

Mika Mathews

ISBN (Print Edition): 978-1-66786-314-6

ISBN (eBook Edition): 978-1-66786-315-3

Contents

The First Fall

"Where am I?"

"Jamestown Hospital," a woman answered, making him turn and blearily look through the harsh silvery light cast by the werelights. The woman was tall and dark-skinned with extremely tight curls that rose in a thick afro around her head. She had high cheekbones and soft, wide lips decorated in purple lipstick. She was stunningly beautiful, and the symbol of a rod with a snake wrapped around a rod branded in her collar bone indicated that she was a High Priestess of Aslcepsius. "We were lucky to manage to save you, dear boy."

He nodded, his mind a blank. "How did I get to Jamestown, which is so far from Bolivar?"

"You were rushed here with all of the refugees."

The boy sat up, ignoring the rush of wooziness. "Refugees?"

"There was an attack. As you are well aware, a fierce civil war is raging among the Gods, and many cities have been caught in the middle of it. A bombing hit your home. There is nothing left, I'm afraid." Her tone shifted, turning soft and sweet but unendingly sad.

The boy slumped. "My foster mom?"

Being a foster kid, separated from anyone who should have cared for him, had been hard enough. His foster mom, Rose, had been one of the few that were half decent toward him. Losing her wasn't hard, but it wasn't entirely an easy loss.

"There were only forty survivors, and you were one of them. I am afraid no one has come to claim you... You had no ID on you. What is your name? "

"Dante."

"No last name?"

"My parents were not wealthy enough to afford one."

Of course, that was not entirely true. His father made more than enough money but chose to give the family name to the woman he remarried and her children. Even Dante's blood siblings, who lived with his father, still did not have a family name. His father was a cruel, selfish man who only cared for his wife.

She nodded. "I figured that would be the case. Bolivar was an impoverished area, and only a few had a family name. You can choose to stay here in Jamestown or be moved to New Olympus with many other refugees. The higher death count in the war and the high recruitment rate mean there are a great many jobs needed to be filled in New Olympus, so you would not be forced into extreme poverty, and you will be safer with the protective barriers around New Olympus." Her tone was sad, knowing the status of their era.

Sighing, the boy nodded. "I will move to New Olympus."

She grabbed his hand. "For what little it is worth, I am so sorry for your loss. I will fill out the paperwork."

As she left, the boy finally managed to mourn Rose's loss. They may not have been close, but he had held her in high regard. That was enough to mouth.

What am I going to do? I was not born to magic. I was not born to a noble bloodline... nor has anyone declared me a priest in training. The heights I can grow are limited; even the military would never accept me. I am too unathletic and fat. The boy poked his belly, seeing the stocky frame despite his poverty, something he inherited from his birth mother. *I am only fourteen, which means most jobs are out of my realm, and I am too old to be adopted by most people. What path is ready for me? What path do I have a chance to fulfill?*

The tears would only stop when the Doctor returned with his release form and a train ticket to New Olympus, which he would board the next day. He would never be ready, but at the end of the day, he really had no choice. Choice was no longer an entity he would have, at least for a long time...

New Olympus

The train ride to New Olympus took twelve hours, with a stop once per hour to let people off at the various towns and cities on the way to the legendary city. Dante, sitting in the low-class section, was squashed next to two burly men on their way to business. He was stuck next to the window, giving him a direct view of the outside world. He saw the ins and outs of the many valleys and rivers, the land wounded from war and healing from centuries of human pollution from the time before the gods returned from their first major war, before they took over the human world, subjugating the people into nothing much more than servants and playthings.

That was fifty years ago, before his mother was even born, in the year twenty-thirty of the old system. Everyone knew the history of the world from that point on; the gods made sure it was plastered everywhere. The gods had descended from their realms, having finally healed up from their war in their own world, only to be fought by mortals refusing their divinity. With powerful weapons, humans fought, only to lose badly. The gods decimated the world at large, reducing humans from eight billion strong to a mere billion. Many lines were lost, and many countries were eliminated.

The gods, as they did in ancient times, helped humans to repopulate. Countless demigods and legacy lines were conceived over the next fifty years, usually from Priest or Priestesses of certain gods, of which Dante's family had never been a part. All seemed well for the first twenty years. The gods healed the Earth from their attack and the pollution of past humans, only for war to break out as the gods broke into factions, desiring power.

However, realizing their powers would decimate the human world, they had humans fight their wars like chess pieces. Priests, shamans, witches, demigods, and so on. Anyone they felt could fight. Anyone born to magic was recruited to fight in the war. The only blessing Dante felt in his life was his inability to be recruited, even if that life was the only one that would present a low-born child with the means to rise up to happiness and peace eventually...

New Olympus was in fact born of these collective facts. New York City, once a vibrant and powerful city of art and trade, was destroyed in the early days of the war. It was replaced by New Olympus, ruled by the Greek Goddess Hera and her lover, the Norse God Baldur. The center of North America, which had been allowed to keep its old name, was home to most of the nobles, high-borns, demigods, and scholars. It was the center of trade and art and magic, like the old New York that it had been built atop. It had the best schools, healers, libraries, and so on.

Dante, despite himself, was in fact excited to arrive at the city. Being an avid reader like his mother, he knew so much about the city. New Olympus was a layered city separated into three descending rings, with the lowest point and ring being the place the poor people lived and where he would be staying. The middle city was for high-born people and the most basic of the temples. The last ring was for gods, demigods, heroes, and nobles. His grandparents had at one point lived in the middle ring, though just barely. Sadly, illness and age had them sent to the outer circle. They died in poverty, leaving the city toward the end of their lives, separating from each other.

To come back to the city now was odd for him, like closing the circle of his ancestry, something he never gave too much thought to.

What was really exciting about the city was the layered protection of each ring. Though weakest on the outer ring, each one was protected by layers of spells. The inner ring was impenetrable as it was cast and secured by the gods, but the outer ring was still incredibly safe. Though he could not remember the attack on his old home, which cost him his mother, Dante felt reassured that he would be safer in his new residence.

According to the doctor, whose name he did not remember, as he was really poor with names, he already had a job and an apartment in the outer ring. A local library serving an entire district and all its schools required someone to clean and monitor it after hours. He would be paid a living wage if he did so, living in the apartment above the library. He had been told flat out that he would be likely required to work extra hours just to get by. So was the world they lived in, that a mere child would be forced to live a life of hard labor despite his young age.

Hours passed, and finally, the city of New Olympus appeared, beautiful and massive, with the first ring firmly in the crater of the old New York, and each continuous ring lifted off the ground in a statement of dominance and superiority. Dante would likely never leave the outer ring, at least not for any reason that revolved around rising through the ranks of life. He was more likely to flee it for one reason or another if the war continued to escalate.

The city has silver towers with runes of all shapes and sizes emanating from them, only to flood the city sky, warping the air like a wave of heat. Even without magic, he could feel the radiant energy oozing from the place; his hairs rose and his skin tingled. He felt a flush wash through him, like rising from warm water into the cool air. It was amazing, the pure power that the gods could wield in the material world.

"We are arriving at New Olympus station. Thank you for choosing Olympus Travels!"

Standing alongside half of the others, Dante followed the long line with his bag of meager belongings, to the exit of the train and onward. Pulling, he saw a cart with a sign that said "Boliver Refugees!" and sadly joined them.

"Where are you heading?" a man with tanned skin asked as Dante walked toward the cart.

Turning toward him, Dante smiled. "Inheritance library in sector four."

"Alrighty, get on and get ready. That's not too far from here."

Getting into the crowded cart, Dante moved down the bumpy unpaved roads into the city proper, where he would make his life his own in the poorest circle of the greatest God-owned city in America.

Inheritance
Library

The library hiring Dante was not as poor as he would have guessed. It was three stories tall and light blue with a black tiled roof. There was nothing particularly impressive about it, but that it was so well built in the poorest district was a good sign as to its value. Hopping off the cart that had carried him from the train station, Dante moved toward the building and headed inside. As he entered the building, he felt a shiver, like cobwebs washing across his skin. It was a familiar feeling, created by the effect of wards registering anyone that crossed them.

"Ahh, you must be Dante."

He almost jumped, the deep, scratchy voice of a man startling him. Turning, he saw its source, a tall man with broader features and an even broader frame. Standing at six feet tall at the least, the man was thick in all definitions of the word. His skin was oddly tanned for one that worked indoors, and he had a bushy beard overgrown on his face.

"Yes, sir," Dante replied, more than a tad nervous.

The man smiled. "Name is Derrek. Nice to meet you. Can't tell you how long it's been since I had a proper custodian here. Few are willing to take up the job. It does not pay the best but you do get a free place to live upstairs."

"How about the books, can I read them?"

Derrek's eyes went wide. "You can read?"

"Yes, my mom taught me. We come from a previously wealthy family."

"I see… Well then yes, just make sure it is not while you are on duty. You may take whatever you like, bar what is under seal." He gestured to the books behind him, directly behind the man behind the desk he was sitting at. There was a bronze cage that seemed to be radiating heat. "It is spelled so that only magic users and approved beings can enter. Magic is illegal to learn without divine blood or divine say-so. That includes the magic books not under seal. Even touching that cage could prove fatal. Be very careful."

Dante shivered. "I will keep that in mind… What are my duties then?"

Happily, Derrek led him through the library, gesturing to what needed to be cleaned by mop or rag or what have you. "And you need to place the books back, straighten desk and chairs, and so on."

There were six rooms on two levels, not counting the bathrooms. All that had to be cleaned from ten at night to six in the morning. Dante felt confident that he could do this all. It wouldn't be exactly easy. There were a lot of things to clean, but he knew he could do it. And if he got the chance to pick up some books to read… then all the better, right?

And maybe I can sneak some magic books… Not all of the magic books are sealed, so maybe…

It would be a great risk but one he was willing to take. Magic was something he craved, from years of reading stories on gods and myths to making his own stories to deal with the loneliness that came from being a social outcast. He was one of the only pure mortals in his old life, most were legacies and demigods of lesser gods and nymphs, so many had shunned him for being a pure mortal. The urge to learn the craft was something he could scarcely imagine not trying.

The tour of the library ended with him being shown his bedroom, a small five-by-ten room with a bed and a dresser, and that was it...

"It's not much," Derrek said, "but it's yours."

Dante nodded. "You are choosing to sponsor me. I cannot argue with this. It is more than enough. Maybe I can one day buy a desk."

"Maybe one day, yes you can. When do you want to start?"

"Tonight is fine. Get me used to the late shift."

"Wonderful. Since no one is here, I can get you your uniform and name tag and show you where the supplies are."

Time would pass fast for Dante over the next two weeks. Getting used to the night shift was hard, as well as the exhaustion born from working for eight hours. He basically just ate, worked, and slept for the entire two weeks. At least until the first New Moon since he started working at the Inheritance Library, where he finally felt awake enough to do something more than the basic parts of living. He started to hoard books.

"Five at a time, kid," Derrek said at the excitement in his eyes.

"I'll be good, sir," Dante replied.

He found and made a mental list of at least fifty books he wanted to read, but he only took five, all on fantasy and magic, though only the stories, not practice. It allowed him to give meaning to his life, to make the days and nights less tedious. He felt finally some sort of peace doing this—living like this—which naturally emboldened his impulsivity and gave him the courage to do something stupid.

Tiptoeing as he cleaned, wiping down the mahogany shelves and dusting the books, he walked into the section on beginners' magic. The first book was small and leather-bound, maybe the size of a small dictionary. It radiated power, like heat off of the pavement, strong enough that he could feel it.

Shaking, he grabbed the book, ignoring the jolt of energy into his skin. "I can read for ten minutes, then I have to get back to cleaning..."

And so he started to read, and the words sank into his skin and his soul.

The Power of Choice and Magic

A true mage is not defined by power but by skill and the ability to choose what path to walk. It is true that a countless many, be they demigod or mortal, believe that true power was something you were born with. This could not be less true. So many have altered their paths by making powerful choices, opening one door or closing another.

It is the power of choice that has allowed those that practice magic to become great. An example of this can be seen between Asclepius and Medea. Asclepius, God of Healing and son of Apollo, actually managed to surpass his father in healing and craft a potion to resurrect the dead due to choosing the path of being a healer over all things.

Medea, a legacy of the Titan Helios and High Priestess of Hecate, actually nearly rivaled his powers in healing through the use of dark magic allowing her the means to even revive dead animals. Medea, a mere legacy actually rivaled someone literally born to heal and was destined to become a god of healing, and Asclepius managed to surpass his Olympian father in an area that was vital to his identity.

Such is the power of choice, in this case, choosing to dedicate oneself to one's goals and tasks. Be it in battle, in enchantment or potion-making, healing, or casting the darkest of curses, this holds true. Never forget it, for this is the center of magic.

Choice, dedication, and knowledge...

Shaking, Dante stood tall. "Choice...? Then this is my choice. I choose to be the best. I will be a sorcerer and no one will stop me. But can I do it alone?" Biting his lip, he closed his eyes. "Hecate, Goddess of Magic and Witchcraft and so many other things... I am but a mere human, please help me. I want to be great, to serve the world, to leave it better than I found it. I cannot do that as I am. I wish to be more, to be better. Please, help me in this endeavor... Help me. Help the world."

There was no flash of light, no magic energy that filled the world, no sign that anyone had heard him in any way, and so Dante sighed as despair overtook him. Solemnly, he closed the book and walked away...

He stopped, suddenly, as something clinked against the ground. Turning, he saw on the tiles a small silver coin. It was twice the size of his thumbnail. Reaching for it, he saw it held a symbol on its front, that of two torches intersecting.

The mark of Hecate.

Shaking with excitement and awe, he touched the coin, and power exploded through his weak mortal flesh. Hot and cold at once, pure magic surged through every cell and with it a deep, melodious voice—that of a woman, three women, speaking at once.

Serve me well, young Acolyte and I will honor your request.

Rising, he realized the coin was on a silver chain. He placed it around his throat and felt the power throbbing through him.

"Why me?"

There was a fluttering of laughter echoing around him.

You asked for it. I am the Goddess of Paths, of choices made. I cannot turn away one that took such a risk for knowledge. Now rise and take up the torches presented to you. Carry them and light your way as my acolyte. Prove your worthiness as my eventual priest. Learn from the book before you, then learn from the sealed books. Find your own path, your own success, as all those that serve me must. I will never hold your hand. You must light your own way through the world with the tools presented.

My blessing in that coin will last but one month, til the next New Moon. By that time, if you prove yourself having gained the power to feel and wield magic without my aid, I will have you extracted as a Priest in Training. Do not prove my choice to aid you a false one, or you will suffer the consequences of that failure...

The voice faded as did the magic in the air, leaving Dante stunned and excited and more than happy. "Thank you for giving me a chance, Hecate. I am not sure how, but I will do my damnedest to make it up to you... now and for as long as I can," he said.

Tucking the coin into his shirt, he quickly went back to work, determined to make the most of the opportunity granted to him, the opportunity he never saw coming. He would make the most of it, and he would rise beyond the sad fate he had been born to. No one would stop him. Not a single damn soul...

A New Acolyte

Magic was a strange thing; it was a mixture of contradictions, cold and hot, powerful and weak, light and dark. When Dante put his hands on his talisman, Hecate's blessing made manifest. He felt all of that at once. Sitting on his bed, he focused on that power and the notes he took from the book of magic, hopeful that he could make manifest the promise he made to Hecate just a few hours past.

"I will make my promise true, Hecate. I have wanted nothing more…" He heard no response from the Goddess, but he had a feeling she was listening. Turning back to his notes, he read quietly in his head.

> *Magic requires unity from three forces, which is why Hecate is the Triple-Faced Goddess. Mind, body, and soul are the sources of all power. The soul grants emotional power and channels the magic. The body endures the power and stores the magic in the flesh. The mind directs the power and gives it purpose.*
>
> *Naturally, there are deviations, like emotion-controlled magic and magic inherited from the body as is seen in Demigods and*

legacies and those blessed with magic via bloodline or destiny. However, when practiced by a true caster, these forces unite and channel the radiant energy present in the world, and infuse it with greater potency, creating magic.

As a new caster, you must use the medium you were granted via blessing or birth to master your craft. Such mediums include divine blood, blessings, or talismans. Using that medium will allow you access to radiant energy until you can fully access magic using the three forces instead of relying on one singular medium such as blood or a talisman. Eventually, exposure to Radiant Energy and Magic will change the vessels and pieces within, creating a greater whole, allowing for greater powers still.

To tap into magic, you must first focus on your medium and then pull radiant energy through the air, where magic from the Godly Plane flows and imbues into all things. Eventually, you will not need this except for the greatest of spells, as your very breath will infuse you with enough radiant energy. Until then, pull it from the air and imbue it intentionally with mental and spiritual strength.

Poetry and rhymes can help focus spells but are technically unneeded. They are mere tools; they help channel intent and sharpen the direction of the mind. When casting your spells, keep this in mind. Think of these things as training wheels, cast aside as you grow in skill and power enough to channel pure will to maneuver mystical forces.

Be warned, magic comes at a cost, even to the strongest... be it blood, stamina, or far worse. Never forget that.

Obeying the book, Dante gripped his talisman, the Silver Coin of Hecate given to him by the Goddess just a few hours passed. Focusing with all his will, he reached out into the air and combed through it. Instantly, something happened... Energy shot through his body into his fingertips and a magnetic pull boiled under his skin. Instantly silvery energy blossomed into existence and he felt its power. It was cold, his skin felt like he had walked out of a bath into the winter air. Goosebumps covered his forearm.

Twisting his hand, he pulled more and more energy out into this plane. Once it was glowing and casting shadows in his room, he knew it was time. Turning to his desk, he focused his will on the small flower on his desk. It was from the front desk, one Derrek insisted be there. It was wilted and weak, but it smelled nice so he took it before it could be thrown away. The flower was white and round with red in the center like drops of blood.

Gather as one, magical light. Render new this flower, return it to right...

With that as his focus, a spell of his own creation, he touched the flower and imagined it slowly returning to life. The wrinkles softening, the brown crusts fading, and the colors bleeding back into their beauty. His head ached with the focus as the silvery energy slowly infuses with intent, and his poem sank into the flower, making his vision come true. And then he felt it, the world swirling and a massive drain on his stamina. He collapsed on his back, breathless.

Magic did indeed come at a cost.

Shaking, he waited a few moments, trying to recover only to realize he was hungry as hell. "Damn... I need to eat..." He sighs. "This is going to be an expensive habit. Magic... Holy hell!" He gasped, looking at the flower. It was now fully beautiful and radiant. He put it in a small cup of water. "I guess I have to do something with this. What could I... Wait, I have the perfect idea." Closing his eyes, he prayed, "Hecate, I have no idea how this works. I have no shrine or temple to make this offering, but this flower touched by my first act of magic, I offer it to you in thanks and also as proof of my promise to work hard. Please accept it."

Before he could open his eyes, there was a whooshing sound, like wind on feathers. Looking, he saw there was no flower in sight, it was entirely gone. Hecate had accepted his offering and he felt damn good about that.

A smile crossed Hecate's face as she held the flower—the peony given to her from her newest Acolyte—close to her face. It was a sweet gesture, a rare one. Hepheastus' followers often did something similar; they offered their first craft to him. She knew her newest follower had no concept of that but had felt the urge to brag and prove his value. As a pure human, he lacked the respect of others and wanted to prove himself.

He has more to lose than most, but he may very well serve me better than a countless many. Her mind and soul cooed with pleasure and pride as she considered what had happened when she watched the boy cast magic for the first time. *His mind and soul are strong, compensating for his weak mortal flesh. He could very well become a great witch, a powerful sorcerer despite his bloodline or lack of destiny.*

Turning away from her mirror, enchanted to give her a view of whatever or whomever she wished to see, she turned back to her temple, where her many priests and priestesses were puttering about, casting spells, gathering strength, and generally preparing for the constant conflict that was to come.

She hated it, the war between her fellow immortals. It had cost a great many of her chosen, be they children or her worshippers, their lives. She wanted to smite Hera, whose cruelty and inability to let go of a grudge had sparked yet another conflict. She was as bad as Zeus had been before he fell during Ragnarok. There was no rightness in forcing mortals to fight for them, and yet that is what their new oaths forced after Ragnarok nearly ended their immortal species. She had foolishly agreed to those oaths out of a moment of fear and weakness, never realizing how much she would regret it.

In many ways, it was why she chose to allow Dante into her service, to prove himself. She could never deny someone the means to better themselves, to make greater choices, to become magical. It was her weakness and always had been. She never approved of destiny, taking free will away was an evil and weak thing.

She could not wait until the boy proved himself, one way or another. She could barely see his future as it was. He was too independent to easily foretell. It made things far more interesting. She wondered deeply what he would make of himself. And yet, she would not put too much effort or time into his path. She would not give power or hold his hand; it was not her way. She would give him tools and help him carve his path, but at the end of the day, it was Dante that would have to make his way to her.

Choice was everything, even in this, and as the Goddess of Crossroads, that was her way...

Midnight Stroll

D ante had always enjoyed the night. Walking under the delicate light of the moon was a pleasure that few could take from him, even in the Third District where the most crime happened in New Olympus. He was jumpy and nervous. Naturally, it was a dangerous time to be awake, even for a bigger guy like him. However, despite that, the urge to be outside walking was too strong.

Looking skyward, he saw the sliver of the moon visible in the night sky. It was three days after the New Moon, and so the light was rather dim, which naturally gave Dante an idea.

Looking in all directions, he offered an emotional prayer to Hecate. He held fast to his talisman and sifted through the air for traces of radiant energy emanating from the Godly plane.

"I call to thee, pure witches fire. A light to lead is my desire..."

Ever grateful for his love of poetry, he quickly cast the spell, creating a small sparkly silver moon all his own, to lead him safely through the bumpy, unpaved road of the Third District. The light, a werelight, danced around him and radiated thin beams, rendering it just a bit easier to see.

Smiling, he cautiously headed down the road, drinking in the moonlight and presence of the radiant energy around him. The drain was minimal, he felt it like a sudden release, like stretching a tight limb or slowly breathing out when one feels stressed. He was slowly exhaling strength, and his soul tingled from the attempt. He knew that one day this would not be the case; expelling this kind of magic would be effortless, even for a weak mortal. And so he walked, but ever once did he realize the eyes of his almost patron goddess were upon him.

It was effortless for Hecate to follow the trace of mortal magic imbued with strength and focus by her blessed talisman, to find Dante as he walked through the Third District. With sacred power, she masked her steps and walked through the shadows to end up behind the boy, with her eyes close on him. She smiled as the boy walked, proud of the simple werelight spell he had crafted. Some casters used dead languages like Latin to cast spells. The boy used the universal tongue and poetry for his. She had read his mind before when he first made his prayers to her and knew that he was a poet by heart. It should have been an easy thing to guess he would use to focus his magic.

She could not wait for the day he did not need such things to cast magic—when his will and emotions were enough to cast spells. It would take some time though, sadly. The boy was her most interesting follower at the moment. The others were walking in ruts and worshipping her, but the boy was learning actively, and for selfish and selfless gain, he was simply more fun to see.

For what felt like an hour, she walked alongside the boy, casting her own dark shadow to make sure he was not discovered for using magic, but allowing him to express his powers. That came to an end when a ghost—a powerful ghost—appeared. They radiated a dull grey light, as all ghosts did, sapping the world of power, absorbing energy from around them to maintain their corporeal forms.

"Hey kid, you're not an approved mage, are you?" the ghost said, making Dante jump, shaking.

"I wonder what he is going to do," Hecate said to herself as she watched.

Dante breathed out and turned to face the ghost, one of many in New Olympus. "I am approved. Hecate gave me her blessing." He pulled out his coin and the ghost's form shivered. He felt the effect, too. Hecate was Queen of Ghosts alongside Melione, and she was also the Goddess of Necromancy, so the ghost could feel her power. "She is your lady. I would advise you not to piss her off. She wants me to study in secret, to prove myself, so I would advise you behave yourself and keep your tongue to yourself."

Hecate laughed, clapping in her shadows. "Very good. Never back down. Ghosts gain their power through bullying it from others. Stand up to that being and take any strength from it before he can take it from you."

The ghost's form shivered again, and then a smile crossed its face. "I like you. Name's Alex. I died here; stabbed to death by a local idiot. What's your name?"

Dante smiled back.

Hecate sensed a connection forging, making her eyes widen. *Does he have a talent for necromancy? Is his will strong enough for such powers?* Pleased, she watched as Dante held out his hand.

"Dante. No last name. Acolyte of Hecate and caretaker of the Inheritance Library," Dante replied.

"Well, Dante, if you ever want some company, just ask..." the ghost smiled. "Hey, I can help you with your magic. I can make it so people won't discover you."

"Why are you being so nice?"

"I like your honesty. You stood your ground, even if slightly. Trust me, people are so afraid of ghosts that they tend to ignore their own needs. They just suck up to us, seeing us as holy or terrifying. It's rather isolating. Loneliness doesn't just affect the living you know."

Hecate sighed, knowing as the Queen of Ghosts just how right he was. Absently, she wondered as they walked away. *Can Alex see or sense me in this disguise? He is rather powerful. Hmm, might have to keep an eye on him, especially if Hades and Persephone really do pull their support like the ocean gods already have...*

Weaving power from her core, she blew it at Alex, binding him to his word with simple necromancy. He could not and would not reveal Dante's secrets. The boy deserved to pass or fail her test in peace.

Alex's presence invigorated Dante, leaving him with a smile and a sense of hope. It was nice sharing his secret with at least one being.

"How long have you been around?" he asked the ghost.

Alex sighed. "Three years, give or take."

"Why are you so powerful? I am new to the craft, and I can feel your power."

The ghost stopped for a moment, giving Dante a full look at him now that the mist-colored light had faded enough to see through. The man was tall, well-built with dull blue eyes and black hair. Sadness was etched into his every feature, even his laugh lines. He must have been nearly forty before he died.

Alex turned to him. "I was mortal. My son was a demigod. My power—what drew Aphrodite to bear my son—was my strong will. The key to magic is also the key to my power."

"Huh..." Dante frowned. "Do you see your son? As an eventual priest, I could find him for you and..."

"No." Alex's tone bore such finality that it stunned Dante into silence. "My son was vapid, cruel, and he mocked my mortality. He knew I died and never visited me or had me buried. It's why I'm still here. But enough of that... You and I have work to do."

Placing his hand near Alex, Dante pushed a feeling of acceptance through his touch as if casting a spell. "If that's what you need, how can you help me mask my magic until I'm ready?"

"Ghosts feed on excessive energy in the air. I can do that for you by consuming the residual magic you leave behind. I get power. You get safety. We both win. Do we have an accord?"

A rush of power suddenly filled the air that left Dante cold, like a reverse furnace, sapping strength and light and warmth.

Knowing it would be binding, Dante nodded. "It is."

The air rippled with the force of their oath. A pact was forged...

Infernal Lessons

"Are you sure about this? The book doesn't mention this."

Alex sighed, smiling at his new living ally. "Dante, I am an incarnation of magic. I know magic better than any book. My every move is an expression of magic, not the body part but mind and soul."

Dante bit his lip and nodded. "Okay..." Sifting through the air, he pulled out radiant energy and let it pool into his hands without crafting a spell. "What now?" As he spoke, the energy sank into his hand, which glowed a soft silver.

"Grab the lock you bought and unlock it, not with a spell but by using sheer focus and will to maneuver the lock within. This will teach you focus and concentration and help you direct your power with more potency. It will also help you when you develop the ability to tap into the radiant energy turned magic pool in your cells and soul."

Dante nodded. His eyes became wide and filled with so much passion and excitement that it hurt Alex to see. Never had anyone, even his son, looked at him like that. "Thank you, Alex." He grabbed the lock and focused, all the while Alex started to whisper behind him.

"Think of it like a magnet in your hand, focused on a single part of the lock. This is the key to telekinesis, typically drawing on the residual power in your cells, but in this case, from the magic you pull from the air. Sharpen your will, your focus, and move the mechanism."

Dante nodded, sweat breaking out across his brow as the magic took its toll. Minutes passed but slowly, and surely the lock opened. He dropped it, panting, with the widest eyes. "I did it!"

"Yes, you did!"

Dante beamed at Alex, his eyes filled with light and life and happiness so strong that it radiated throughout the room. As a being that drew strength from energy—all energy—Alex could literally taste it. It was like pure ambrosia to a sorrowful soul, but also painful, like spicy food on a delicate tongue.

It was hard not to love the boy, whose aura was solid, strong but filled with muted life. Alex could tell Dante rarely expressed his full self but held a rare zest for life. Though they had only known each other for about a day, the "father" in Alex saw a "son" in Dante, something his ghostly obsession, the anchor to his soul, found nauseatingly addictive. He ached to nurture the boy, to guide him, to protect him. It was in truth the very reason he agreed to help the boy before. He just had to obey the obsession anchoring him to this plane, but in truth, he would have done it anyway. The boy just clearly needed a guiding hand, and damn it if Alex would not be just that, even if they just met.

"Alex, what else can I do with this?" Dante gestured to the light still in his palm.

Alex smirked. "Want to see a silver flame?"

A hauntingly awed look crossed Dante's eyes, and Alex knew he had the boy hooked.

Hecate cackled loudly, watching her newest acolyte generate fire from sheer radiant energy. The ghost was a good mentor, kind and helpful with good intentions. Reading into his heart had been easy enough. With his help, the boy was almost ensured to becoming a Priest and Sorcerer. She was excited about this; the entire notion was something she could not wait for.

"The boy's future is becoming clearer as his choices create a path for me to see. Something to anchor to..." Tapping her purple nails against her chin, she focused harder, and the boy's path started to come into focus. It was still murky and hard to see but the raw progress he was making was forging something new. The entire thing seemed brighter. The shapes were more defined, the images less murky. There were several paths; however, the most dominant one radiated deep violence and fear that caught her attention in a way she did not like. It was a new violence, one not familiar to her. "What could it be? Please Hades, Persephone, do not launch your own fight against the Domestic Deities as Poseidon and his ilk have. This world is being torn apart enough. Just look at Dante, he is only in New Olympus because of an attack on his hometown. Enough with this violence."

She sighed knowing that, as the only deity with a finger in all realms, other than Iris and Hermes, she was doomed to play a part in the war, no matter who turned against who, and naturally that meant her children, priests, and lovers.

If only she could stop it all. If only...

"I need an Ambassador to walk the dark paths and speak to Hades and Persephone, to convince them to stay on the right path, to not rebel against the Domestic Deities, the heavenly gods. Perhaps someone to convince the b#tch Hera to cool down and stop insulting everyone. If only. If only..."

Grabbing another flower from Derrek's wilting vase, Dante held it in his glowing hand. Slowly, he pushed the magic into it, not casting a spell at all. To his amazement, the magic took instant effect, and the flower, a rose this time, started to revive and perk up. A smile crossed his face.

"This is how I heal people, too?"

Alex, who was watching from the side, nodded. "Yes, it is. Only small wounds, to trying to stem the tide of blood. A spell might be better for bigger wounds."

Dante sighed. "I really want to heal. I think it would be good for me..."

"You seem the type."

"I think we should practice this more."

"We have almost a month to kill. Let's see what you can do, kid. I want you to be a full mage by the next New Moon!"

Dante nodded, excited and afraid but ultimately ready...

Shattered

One week since finding the Coin

"Ahh!" The screams of terror shattered any trace of sleep from Dante's soul, tearing him straight from dreamland and into a world of horror. Eyes wide, the world was framed in red and dread.

"Fire!" He threw himself out of bed, rushing out of his room and down the stairs to the library, where he saw Derrek shivering behind his desk.

"Don't think about it, kid!" the man called out over the screams. "Something broke through the third barrier. This place has some protective magics over it, but outside, you are entirely boned."

Dante shivered, fear overtaking him for a moment. And then he heard it... A scream. A child's scream.

His mind made up, all fear faded out. *Hecate, guide me if I matter to you at all... Help me... Help them!* Shaking his head, Dante turned to a nearly see-through Derrek. "I don't care. Someone needs to help." He rushed out, past the barrier of magic that protected the library and into the disaster that was the Third District. Blood was everywhere; people running and screaming from fire and pulsating magics. Turning, Dante saw the source of their fears.

It was massive; a writhing mass of tentacles and hate, a nasty sickly grey and yellow. Every time it waved its tentacles, waves of heat radiated from it and something caught fire. Only the fire was redder than a normal fire, and it oozed magic. Hate filled Dante at the sight of it.

"What the hell did we do to you, whoever sent this freaking thing?"

Shaking his head, he turned and saw a child held by his father, screaming in agony as horrible burns covered his face. It was to him that Dante ran, hoping his week of magical training would be enough for him to save this child. Grabbing his talisman, Hecate's blessed coin, he pulled power into his hand and chanted, *"Blessed powers, holy light. Heal this child, make this right!"* With hope and fear as his drive, ignoring the monster destroying everything, he put his glowing hand on the child, nearly fainting as his lifeforce tanked from his first healing. Shaking away the black spots, he looked up at the grateful father. "Run!"

The man nodded, gripping his son tightly before darting off as fast as he could, leaving Dante to continue his work.

Dante found another person to help, a woman pinned by rubble. With his large frame, it was easy to push it off, his muscles only slightly screaming. Swatting away the dust, he put his hands on the woman's leg, pushing in power and watching the bleeding wound slowly close up. "Get to safety."

The woman obeyed him, rushing off to safety.

This went on for a while. Dante would find a person, heal the person with raw magic or a spell, and then send them off. No one questioned him, hit him, or refused his aid. He just worked on and on and on and on. It was only after the fifteenth person that he realized something odd...

Rushing toward two terrified teens a bit older than he was, one writhing from his burns, his mind opened. *How am I healing so many people? Should this be killing me? I am not even tired.* Dante was shaking with power, energy, and strength. He could never remember feeling so mighty! With shaky eyes, he looked down at his hands and realized that he was glowing silver, the light of which was emanating from his talisman in thick waves, sinking into his skin. *Hecate, if this is you, thank you.*

With that out of his mind, he focused and returned to his mission and hurried to the teens. That was when everything went horribly wrong…

A shadow formed around the teens, a tentacle was falling their way, and he knew they would not survive it. Pushing himself harder, he threw out his hands, and Alex's recent lessons took effect. Throwing out his hands, Dante pushed with all his focus, a thousand times greater than when he picked the locks or heal the roses. Emotion dominated his every facet, altruistic energy that exploded from within him in a wave of energy so strong that the magic of Hecate evaporated, the Silver Coin shattered and his lifeforce rushed out of his body, knocking aside the beast's tentacle and banishing its waves of heat.

And then, Dante, the fourteen-year-old pure mortal that he was, fell face-first to the ground… and died. His heart stopped, and all his life force evaporated from his weak, mortal vessel.

Darkness drank him in, drowning him in its thick, viscous essence, and his soul descended into nothingness.

"Foolish boy!"

Dante opened his eyes, startled to see the beautiful unfamiliar beauty of a woman staring at him. She was clearly a goddess, though he wasn't sure how he knew it with her childish appearance. She didn't seem too much older than he was, with skin fairer than white. Her lips were the deepest red, her eyes the darkest green, and her body was covered in a blue dress the color of midnight. She was gorgeous and utterly pissed. A growl escaped her lips and she reached down and pulled him up. "Look around us, what do you see?!"

It was not a question but an order, one he obeyed. Realizing, he saw... nothing! There was nothing, only a vast emptiness with him floating in a vast void. "What, where am I?"

"Nowhere. You are in the space between space, where magic and souls gather to be collected by Death!"

Dante stepped back. "I'm dead... Wait... of course, I am dead. I used up all my lifeforce protecting those kids. At least I made a difference with my life."

The woman sighed, brushing his hair aside. "You are not entirely dead, your heart just stopped. I can restart you. Should I do so in the next few minutes? However, you must know something... You strained your soul, casting such advanced magic. You tried to disrupt a being born of a god's power, and your spell born out of sheer panic and your willingness to suffer worked, barely, but at great cost. Your soul is tremendously damaged, and your talisman is shattered. No magic can restore it. You lost my blessing entirely."

Her sternness and words hit him at once. He tried to kneel but found that he couldn't really do that while floating in the void, so he settled for bowing his head. "Lady Hecate, I didn't know it was you."

She frowned as he looked up. "You wouldn't, would you? Unlike most Gods, I rarely have statues of me carved, so you have nothing to compare me to, other than my children, and they are conceived through three different forms."

He nodded, trying to collect himself. "So umm... why am I here?" He looked up, shaking. "I thought you said I wasn't dead. Not entirely?" He didn't want to be dead, not when there was so much more life to be lived.

Hecate's eyes tightened with pain. "Your soul wandered for a moment. I caught it before it went to the arms of Thanatos. The backlash from your spell rendered you more free-floating, making it easier to catch you." Then she sighed, turning away. "You must be more careful. Too much rests on your shoulders. I will not intervene again. I am not allowed to more than once in an instance like this. Should you fail, your soul will drift endlessly until someone chooses to collect it. Am I understood?"

"Yes ma'am!"

"Good..." Hecate smiled, and then Dante's soul quivered. "You will like what is coming to you when you awaken... Now go and live!" With cold fingers, she flicked his forehead and everything went black again, only this time he felt a rush of agony that was his reentry into life.

Breathing hurt, existing hurt, everything hurt...

Opening his eyes, Dante saw several people bowing over him, tears in their eyes, including Derrek and a very miserable Alex. The monster from before was dead, its rotting corpse was being carted away by a group of people marked with power and magic. The conflict was over.

Realizing why people were crying over him, he lifted his hand. "I am not dead!" he groaned, and they all snapped to him.

"You are alive!" Alex and Derrek said as one.

"Yes, but I was dead for a bit there." Dante sat up, the world spinning for a minute. Oddly, no one tried to help him move. Actually, they were all several feet from him, looking at him as if he was divine. "Umm... why is everyone so far away?"

Alex approached, kneeling. "This." He pointed with his see-through hand, to a mark on Dante's chest, one seared into his skin, black as coal and radiating cold power. It was of two torches, crossing each other. The Mark of Hecate. "You are now a Priest of Hecate... You are now a sorcerer."

"How? It's only been a week."

Alex laughed. "Sacrifice bears powerful magic. Your final act—giving yourself to the magic—was the final key. It awakened your sensitivity."

"Young lord!" They all jumped, turning to see several women approaching with a pallet and medical equipment. One stood out; she was tall for a woman and built thickly with a thin nose, high cheekbones, and light brown hair. She had a quirky smile and a warmth about her. "We were asked to help take you to the temple of Hecate, to be healed."

"Hello," Dante said meekly.

"My name is Brighid, Priestess of Asclepius," she said, her tone loud and strong. "I will be taking care of your healing personally. Oh, and your ghost friend is to come with you. Put him on the gurney."

As Dante was lifted up, cheers radiated outward as people called out in thanks for his work in saving so many lives. The weight of their love was a lot, and before he passed out once again, tears fell down his face as he realized the power of his new purpose and the path that he had chosen.

He no longer served himself, he served everyone.

Paths of Magic

The inner rings were night and day different. The Third District, which he barely saw in the three weeks he was there, was dusty and filled with dilapidated houses and rough roads. The Second District was silvery and powerful, with a barrier so strong that it scrapped against his skin as he was carried through it. It had beautiful houses and shops, well-dressed kids, and everyone had shoes and looked well fed. They bowed to him, just as they had in the Third District.

The First District radiated power; its ring was so powerful that he felt it like walking through a waterfall of steaming lava. Dante cringed in agony as his senses were forced to endure such magic—magic straight from the gods themselves. The district itself had countless temples and towers and stunning mansions. There were a lot of people, oddly, and he saw them with proud smirks looking at him with boredom and expectation. It was the strangest thing, as if he was still beneath them in their eyes.

Hecate's temple was easy to see, for it was directly in the center of the district, right in front of the exit of the Second District. It was massive and radiated her dark power, a wave of cold energy that soothed him, like the soft silvery light of the moon and the cool air of the darkened night sky. It made sense for her to be first. She was the great connecter; all magic came from and through her. She was the Goddess of Crossroads and one of the only gods to hold sway in all Four Realms.

The actual temple was sheer black, with silvery marbled cracks through it. Keys and torches were painted across its walls, which seemed to ripple with waves of magic and heat. Sconces blasting silver flames decorated its sides. There were countless plants around its shade, which seemed darker than average. The doors to the temple were massive and decorated with three women—the three sides of Hecate: Maiden, Mother, and Crone. They were stunning representations, and Dante could not help but feel awe at their sight.

Brighid, as the lead, took him straight inside, where he gasped as sheer magic filled the air, not just radiant energy but pure, potent, cool magic so strong that he felt his body ache with it, his tender wounded soul quivering with the force of it all. His whole body shivered, his eyes, blurring out of focus. And then warmth, like that of the summer sun, radiated through his foot into his body, detaching him ever so slightly from the power of the temple. Turning as his focus returned, he saw Brighid holding his foot, smiling.

"I should have warned you. Not only are you new to sensitivity, but you have never been in a temple. It is pure, focused power from a god, or goddess in this case. Combined it can be overwhelming. Thankfully my powers are enough to help guide your wounded soul through that."

He nodded to her. "Thanks."

"Not a problem."

They continued to lead him through the wintery air of magic, past several rooms and marble pillars, into a room filled with four doors. In the center were two torches and a circle of runes and magical symbols so old that his mind swam with the possibilities of what they meant. They laid him down in the center of the circle, stepping back as a form appeared from the soft torch heat. It was Hecate, and she was smiling down at him.

"Hello, there. It is nice to meet you once more, dear Dante."

Meeting her in person and not just as a spirit, Dante felt the raw power oozing from her, sizzling against his skin. "Same, my lady."

She laughed at the other's gasp, likely at his formal tone. "I always meet my newest priests and chosen children. I cannot ask your loyalty if I am a ruling figure from on high. Today, I will asses you for the power your newly gained magic leads you toward. The magic that, through the unity of mind, body and soul, you will find most connective and appealing. Rise and grab the torches. They will expand your magic outward, and the rooms that light up in this circle will tell us what magics you lean toward. On each door are runes from the ancient languages that will tell me more specifically what magics you lean toward.

"The four doors represent Earth, Heaven, Underworld, and Sea—the four aspects that rule the world. Within each door lies a library with books on the magics that are ruled by those four realms. Necromancy for the Underworld, botany for the Earth, and so on. So, lift my sacred torches and let your power spread. Let us see where you find power!"

Dante, with shaking limbs, managed to stand. Grabbing the torches, which oddly were not hot, he lifted them skyward and felt tremendous but delicate power shoot through him before rippling outward into the world. To his shock and Hecate's, all four doors lit up, though not all were equally bright. Two doors were brighter than the others, by far. He felt their power as they linked with his magic, and he knew their purpose. Runes danced upon the doors, silver naturally, and he felt their purpose as well.

Hecate smiled, radiant as the new moon, and laughed a sound so perfect that Dante's soul danced in response. "Amazing! My boy, with only mortal blood and a righteous will, you have somehow managed to develop a connection to all four realms of magic! All humans are connected to the Earth. You were crafted from clay by Prometheus and were later reborn through Gaia's magic after the flood. And so, you all are tied to the Earth.

However, you also hold great ties, tremendous ties, to the Underworld itself, as strong as your earthen ties. The Seas and Skies, though fainter, are still tied to you.

"From the Earth, you hold connection to healing magic, most potently the energy of creation and life, as well as potion making. From the Underworld, you hold sway with Necromancy, which is my greatest magic, and mediumship. From the Sky, the Heavens, you hold sway with enchantment. From the Seas, your power is connected with divination, a power which all those born with the sea hold sway, especially now since Apollo died during Ragnarok."

Dante frowned. "I thought divination would be a sky power? Same with healing, since both were Apollo's domain?"

Hecate laughed. "He was the best of it, but he was more of an abnormality. All domains can heal or divine or do all magics, but the greatest focus is through the elements I mentioned."

"I see... Thank you."

With a wave of her hand, the four doors opened. "You have access to all magics. I will not restrict you, but be wise, my son, and walk with patient steps. Do not go where you cannot handle it." Hecate bowed to him once and vanished in a swirl of heat that he felt.

Putting the torches down, Dante turned to the collective and saw them bowing as well. Then, one girl detached herself from the rest and rushed to him. She was wearing all black, essentially a pantsuit, and smiled at him. Her skin was impossibly dark, matching her hair with tight curls about her face. She had wide, thick lips curled into a wonderful smile. She was radiant and oozed wisdom and warmth.

"My name is Lenore." Her voice, like all people in the modern world, lacked accent as they spoke the universal language, but there was so much power in her tone, that it bordered on divine. She oozed magic, and he knew she was in charge. "I am the Head High Priestess of the Temple. It is an honor to meet you, Dante. Mother Hecate told me of your potential coming days ago. We never expected to see you so soon, but your virtuous act unlocked your potential powers far earlier than we could have predicted." She grabbed his hands suddenly and hummed a soft lullaby. Dante felt power flood his skin, and cold magic numbed his weariness. "I am an expert in all magics, but healing is where my heart is, as well as combat magic. In honor of your remarkable potential, I will teach you healing personally."

Dante grinned, "Thank you so much."

"Not a problem, my little love. Oh, and your ghost friend Alex will be staying in your room. We have many ghosts here; they thrive in the powerful magic of this place. Never worry for him. He may not be a priest or a child of Hecate, but he holds her and my blessing."

"Again, thank you." Dante turned and smiled at Alex, who nodded with pride in his eyes.

"Now, it is time you get some rest. Only basic magic for the few days until your soul heals more. We will be having healing sessions every day until you recover. I also want you to be studying rather seriously for some ti, what with the most recent attack. You may not have a natural affinity for combat but you need to learn it for your own safety. That includes swordplay or archery. Now, I will lead you to your room. Alex will follow you." She waved to her flock. "Be safe, my darlings, and return to your work."

The crowd dispersed, and so Dante walked away with Alex and Lenore.

"What is our first lesson?"

Lenore beamed. "Not a healing one... you need to make your own personal talisman. It won't give you magic but it will focus your powers, act as an anchor for spells and offer some sort of boost. For example, Lapis Lazuli can offer mental protection and clarity. Ruby can offer courage and increase firey spells. Quartz is tied to the earth and psychic energies. It is used for clarifying and connecting and is great for scrying. Silver is the best metal for connection, channeling magic, and protection. Now, enough of that. Off to bed."

And like that, Dante's day ended early, but with so much power, sleep was nothing but welcome.

A New Mentor

"Get up, kiddo, it is time to go!"

Alex's words managed to draw Dante from his dreamless sleep, courtesy of Lenore's simple spell. He could never remember resting so well. *I feel... great, sore and achy but otherwise great!*

Beaming, he sat up and took a moment to really embrace his massive room. It was so much bigger than his previous room, with a desk and a large bookshelf. Silvery torches filled the room, radiating warmth and power. There was a large closet filled with clothes for him to wear. All were dark colors like black or purple or blue or forest green. Magically tailored for him or so Lenore said the night before. On the far wall was a nice fireplace, radiating warmth and heat and comfort. All in all, it was a lovely room and he could not believe he was in it.

Sliding out of bed, Dante realized he was dressed only in his boxers in front of Alex. He flushed, turning away with shaking limbs covering his body. He hated his body, he always had. He was tall, flabby, thick, pale, and hairy. He was used to mockery and mistreatment for lacking the beauty of those with divinity.

"Kid, it's okay," Alex said, suddenly close to him. Jumping, Dante saw the sad look on Alex's face. "If you are really so uncomfortable with your body, you can always work out. You sort of have to, as a witch practitioner. But honestly, you look fine." His tone was soft, sad but genuinely proud and warm.

Nodding, Dante's hands moved from his body. "Sorry, but in a world of people that look perfect, thanks to their divine blood, I... well, it's not easy."

"Trust me, I know what you mean... Now, get dressed and let's go. Okay?"

Dante nodded and walked off to the dresser, missing the sad, genuinely considering eyes of his ghostly ally.

Lenore rarely dug into her students' minds, but with Dante, she had no choice. The boy's will was so strong that his mind and magic were utterly intertwined. Healing him brought up memories of pain he could not stop with his current mental and magical skills. Her magic, trying to heal him, drew out the painful memories. While she could not have seen them—she had not focused on his memories—she could taste the pain behind them. He had experienced tremendous pain, abuse, mistreatment, hate, self-hate, and so on. She felt that his soul had been hurt from a lifetime of mistreatment; his body had suffered from countless blows, especially his head, which worried her greatly for his future.

However, the most prevalent pain she sensed was a long-running depression, a soul-deep leech on his psyche. The boy was all too aware of it, and though he had been too focused on his life for the depression to have much effect, it would come to the surface soon enough, and that could be dangerous for a magic user. She would have to watch over him, deeply and carefully over the next few years...

The boy in question walked into the room she was in, led by his Ghost, dressed in blue jeans and a forest green hoodie. He looked lovely in her eyes, his face was warm and round and pale, his brown eyes filled with sharp emotion and frightening intelligence. He had a beard growing on his face despite his young age. His hair was soft and curly, shiny and perfect. She knew he had no concept of how adorable he was, how comforting and kind he looked, but that was simply true. He was and would never be perfect, but his good heart and terrifyingly powerful mind rendered him nice to look at.

Smiling softly at the boy, she bowed softly. "Good morning, my love. Did you sleep well?"

The boy nodded. "Thanks to your spell, I did." He smiled. "I can't remember sleeping that well, like ever."

"Healing spells are my specialty, as they will be yours. Speaking off, I have sad news. I cannot help you with your studies today or your talisman, too many were injured in the recent attack. Powerful god magic was imbued in that fire, and I must tend to the wounded. However, a friend and powerful High Priest is free. His name is Naveh, and he is something of a genius in the realm of enchantment. He is actually in the Healing Wing, which is connected to Asclepius and Epione's temple, injured in one of his mad projects. His wounds are recovered enough to be of service to you. Follow me."

Together they marched down the long hall and toward the Healing Wing, which was actually not far from Dante's bedroom. As they walked, she continued speaking to the boy.

"Now, as a Priest and Healer in training, you must serve the temple in some capacity. You will clean the Healing Wing, bath our patients, ambulate them, dress them, and so on. We have no servants here, so these are your duties. Sadly, there are so few healers as most would rather gain glory in combat, so you might be a bit lonely."

The boy shrugged. "I am sure Alex can keep me company as we work."

She nodded. "Likely yes. I should also tell you that there is a reason you are a healer and a necromancer and even a diviner and enchanter. All require a potent will. Enchantment is impressing your will onto an object. Divining is using your will to see through time and space. Healing requires you to sense and deal with the pain of others, as true healing magic forces you to endure and connect to others. Necromancy is about using your will to conquer the dead as Alex can attest to."

Alex nodded in return. "She is right. That is the whole key to my power and to commanding the dead."

She continued, "Remember that, as you make your talisman today. You need to infuse that potent will into the object, so it links to you wholely." They reached the Healing Wing, and with a wave of her hand, velvety magic rippled outward, forcing the barrier to accept her presence. She turned to Dante. "My other specialty, outside of healing and combat, is protective. All wings hold powerful protective magics, and the Healing Wing is the most protected. When you swear your oaths and become a full priest, you will gain access to the libraries and various wings based on your oath. Until then, you need to have someone with you, someone trusted."

The Healing Wing was massive, a long hall with beds on each side and glorious stained glass windows, depicting various scenes on each wall between each bed, granting a haunted cool light to the room. She led the boy past various beds, most filled with sick or injured people moaning out. One bed, six beds past the entrance on the left, held a large, thickly-built, bald man with a potent red, scraggly beard. He was fair-skinned with thick glasses and a scowl on his face.

"When am I getting out of here, Lenore!" he said the moment he saw her, making her laugh.

"In a few minutes, Naveh, but first let me introduce you to your newest student." She turned to Dante. "Meet Dante, our newest Priest in Training. He is pure mortal but shows great promise. I am sure you heard how he saved those many children during the most recent attack."

Naveh turned to the boy and offered a genuinely warm smile. "Nice to meet you, kid. Name's Naveh."

Dante smiled. "Same."

Lenore beamed. "Lovely, you are getting along. Now, Dante, Naveh is the High Priest of Hecate in charge of Crafts and Construction. He is a master builder of all things. He is the first mortal to make an automaton for a very long time." She leaned down and looked at the ground, where a massive grey, white and black dog rested. She reached over and scratched its chin. "This is Nanuk, the said automaton. He has his own soul, something that earned Naveh his spot as High Priest. His specialty beyond being a craftsman is combat magic, which he will be teaching you as well. Magic is learned through studying and doing, and so you need a mentor. He will show you everything and make sure you do not hurt yourself."

Dante nodded. "I look forward to working with you, Naveh."

"Same... Be warned, I expect the best from you. You earned your spot as a Priest despite a lack of nepotism. You must continue to earn your power and position. I earned my spot, despite being a mere legacy of Hephaestus, where several sons and daughters of said god failed to do so. I did that, not them. I will not coddle you or kiss your ass. Understand?"

Dante nodded, looking far happier. "I like that. Thank you."

"Good. So, am I free, Lenore?"

Lenore sighed, rolling her eyes at her beloved friend. "Fine, you are free to go. I read your report this morning. Stay away from your last experiment, and you should be fine. Remember, you need more fireproofing for such dangerous tasks. Your legacy blood may provide you with some protection, but it is not enough."

He scowled. "Fine."

"Now go and help the boy. Your first task is to make his talisman. I expect to be wowed, Naveh. The boy holds connections to necromancy and healing, he needs something rather impressive."

"Of course, I am not an invalid."

Waving her hand, Lenore walked away from the two. "Behave yourselves... Oh and Dante, you are working nightshift here. Come to me around ten at night. That is when you are set to work here. You are set to work three days a week in the Healing Wing. The rest of the time, you are to study until you are good enough to serve as Lady Hecate's Priest."

Dante frowned. "What would I be doing? As a full Priest, I mean."

"Healing here in the wing and stopping those dead creatures haunting the living, those abusing their powers, unlike Alex."

Alex shuddered. "So many of us are harming the living, Dante. So, so many. I have seen people killed by ghosts, haunted to madness, or just annoyed. So many need to be stopped."

"Wow! That is heavy. Worth it, but heavy."

Naveh nodded. "It can be, serving the gods... Now come on, it's time to get you started. And frankly, I can't wait to get out of this place."

With that, they hurried off, leaving Lenore to sigh at them.

What am I going to do with Naveh...? He'll be back here in a week. I just know it. Knowing she had work to do, Lenore pushed that from her mind, pulled up her sleeves, and swiftly got started doing what she did best.

Crystal Gifts

It was hard for Dante, a slow walker, to keep up with Nevah. The man was practically sprinting out of the Healing Wing. His stride was really long; he was booking it. His dog automaton, which looked like a real dog, was making equal pace with his master. Its stride was smooth and flawless, like a real dog and not a machine, adding to his awe at the mechanical beast.

After a few minutes of misery, they reached a long hall oozing power and heat, literally in waves that shimmered in the air. Nevah stopped by the entrance, turning to Dante to press his forefinger against the young boy's forehead.

"I allow you entrance!" Nevah chanted. A spark of power shot through Dante, making his new tattoo shiver. "That should give you access to my realm. Now follow me and observe my people."

As they walked in, the clamoring sound of people at work echoed in the hall, clings of metal, the scent of wood and metal being seared, and the breath of magic oozing its way through the air. It gave Dante, whose soul still ached, a bit of a headache. Through various open doors, he saw people pounding on forges, working over desks, stitching clothes, and tinkering on great machines. It was awe-inspiring to watch, even if a bit confusing.

Alex, who was behind them, shimmered and slowly gained his color back, looking almost alive. He winked at Dante. "Magic like this—crafting spells—create a lot of excess power that I can draw on for a stronger anchor."

"Ah..."

Two minutes later, at the end of the hall, they reached a door that led to an office filled with a bronze desk and tons of half-built things. "This is my home away from home." Nevah boomed, proudly gesturing to the many things around him. "It is where many of our meetings will be. I have a lot to do as a High Priest, so most of the time you will be working on your own. But never think to practice spells or bigger magics without guidance. You could easily overextend yourself and die. You need to be watched over. That is vital." His eyes, a reddish brown, fixed Dante with a command that rivaled that of Hecate's. His words simmered with power that was palpable, making Dante realize a measure of the man's power.

"Yes sir."

"Now, onto your talisman, this is something I have quite a bit of excessive skills on. I am an expert on crafting. I am the great-grandson of Hephaestus, a High Priest of Hecate, and I have melted three talismans of my own in my attempts to improve my own. Nanuk is actually my talisman now, made of adamantine, a gift from my grandfather. You cannot wield a divine metal like adamantine or orichalcum. Your magic is too tied into the Earth for that, but you can use magic. So you need to use a natural metal.

"I have some ideas for you... With silver being your metal, as it is the most powerful natural metal and holds great protective properties, your center will have to be something special. Perhaps a mineral or natural object that can channel your powers properly and grant you some protection. Hmmm... it would have to be really special as you are a necromancer and a healer—contradicting magics. But you also need something to help your weak vessel and to offer you protection in the field if you were to go out and heal those harmed in the greater conflict."

Dante's heart quivered at the idea that he would have to go and be in conflict. He didn't even know why the gods were fighting; few did. All he knew was the violence and suffering it caused. No one, bar the gods and their servants, knew what this war was about. Though as a new priest, it was likely going to be revealed to him.

Shifting his focus, Dante turned back into Naveh's words, finding it more soothing and a safer topic than war.

"Hmmm... Dante, come here." Naveh waved his hand, and one of the shelves erupted into rust-colored smoke. When it faded, there were dozens of drawers filled with objects of all types. "Put your hand out, filled with your focused magic, and you should feel a natural hum of which element focuses your powers best. It is a rudimentary tool, this trick, but it works well. The objects you see here are the ones I suspect will help you best."

Nodding, Dante approached and did as he was told, combing radiant energy into his hands, which glowed its typical silver. Moving it about, he searched for his potential talisman. With each pass, he felt various pulls and heard his mentor making comments on each one.

"No coral... Amber responded well... and so did turquoise," Naveh said.

This went on for a few minutes before Dante stopped as pure cold magnetic energy pulled on his magic. Turning, he saw Naveh looking at him with a smirk.

"Interesting... I should have guessed," Naveh uttered.

Curious, Dante asked, "What is it?"

"Bone," Naveh said. Dante cringed, looking at the bleached objects. "Not just any bone but hellhound bones collected many years ago and purified through powerful ceremonies. We use them for the rare necromantic spells, even Hecate has to use them. I never have made a talisman with them, but it entirely makes sense. They are tied to the Underworld, being the Children of Nyx and Cerebus, but they have the power to live on Earth, something I imagine you know well."

Dante nodded. "Of course, it was why I had to take a train here, why all cities have protective barriers and temples, to protect us from the wild monsters living in the wild. Hellhounds, Empousai, Mania, Karpoi, the new Minotaurs, and the untold beasts created by the curses cast during the war and during Ragnarok."

Naveh smiled. "Exactly. Now, tamed Hellhounds are used to retrieve souls for the gods. They work with the Furies. Wild ones are hunted by Artemis and her hunters, and as they are both Night Goddesses, she gives the bones and pelts to Hecate to use. We make arrows, daggers, and clothing from their remains. It makes them resistant to Underworld magic and dark curses. Your talisman will be rather interesting. Cerebus is the grandson of Phorcyus and Keto, two Sea gods, both of whom were also children of Gaia. He is also the grandson of Gaia, through his Father Typhon, and the grandson of Tartarus, but in actuality, Cerebus takes after Gaia's magic greatly. Though he serves the Underworld, he is a creature of Earth by nature. That makes his children's bones a perfect blend of the two realms. I really should have guessed we would be making your talisman from this material. Now come and let's get started." Naveh grabbed a few pieces of bone and placed them on his desk alongside some silver from another drawer. "I need your blood infused with magic... and your help."

Shaking a little, Dante drew on more magic, not bothering to cast a spell with it. "How do I help?"

"Just focus your will. Enchantment is all about putting your mind, intent, and will into an object, imbuing it with what you want. This is no different." Naveh waved his hand, and a circle of runes appeared, made of the same rusty-colored magic as before. "Quickly now! We don't have all day. I want to get you started on your workouts and combat training. You will be working on that daily for at least an hour and a half, to get you into shape and able to defend yourself with magic if need be."

Dante moved closer to Naveh who, in a flash, grabbed and cut Dante's palm with a knife appearing from nowhere. Dante didn't even flinch, much to Naveh's shock.

"That didn't seem to bother you?"

"I am used to pain."

That seemed to sadden Naveh, who quickly brushed it off. "Let the blood drip onto the talisman pieces and focus your will forward. Your identity, your existence, all you want your talisman to be. That will connect it to you, bind it to you, make it so only you can use its power."

Nodding, Dante did as he was told, all while he watched Naveh do something amazing. Naveh's hands moved in a delicate, controlled motion around the pieces, glowing a strong rust color. The man's magic, charged with intent, fused with the materials as if heating them up. This went on for a few minutes before he clapped, and the magic burst into a large flame that made Dante step back in shock. When the flames vanished, and his vision stopped being blurry with spots, Dante saw something incredible... His talisman was finished and utterly gorgeous.

Shaped like a tear, the silver wrapped around the bone and held a spiral pattern etched in blood red. It was held on a chain that glistened with magic. Without hesitating, Dante reached for it, only to be stopped by Naveh.

"Not yet, as by taking this, you agree to bind yourself to Hecate and to serve her. It is powerful, a magical binding, a mark on your soul. You cannot break your word." As he spoke, his words filled the room with his unbridled power. "Your very existence is tied to her, fueling her with people's thanks. That is how you serve her; your acts give and take her strength. Your word becomes her words, and your deeds are hers. Can you do this? Can you agree to the weight of this path?"

Dante nodded. "Yes, I can."

"Then so be it! Do you, Dante, swear by the River Styx, our most sacred oath, to serve the Goddess Hecate until and after your death, unless she releases you from her path? To never betray her, to act in her stead, to heal and help and guide and follow the path of one of her priests?

The words slammed into Dante, not just with power but the promise they held. He was binding himself forever to a goddess. That was not and could not be taken lightly. And yet he knew his answer.

"Yes, I swear on the River Styx to these terms," Dante answered.

And with those words, he buckled over, holding his head as the magic of Styx wove his oath into his very soul with a cold power beyond anything he would ever know. He knew then, as if by instinct, that if he broke that oath the magic Styx would unravel his very soul. Nothing would be left of him, and if he somehow by some miracle survived, Helios as Guardian of the Oaths would come for him to let out the Gods Justice. He would never know rest or peace or salvation...

The world cleared up as Styx's potent power faded, but the pain of his oath etched into his soul remained. Standing, Dante saw a stoic Alex and Naveh looking at him.

Naveh held out the talisman. "The weight of the oath is nothing to sneeze at, is it?"

"No, I never could have guessed it would be so... cold, painful, and terrifying..." Dante said.

"Styx's powers were always great. When Zeus made her the binder, it changed her and made her greater. She is one of only a handful on par with the Divine Council. Hecate is another, as is Themis the Titanness of Justice and Order, and Persephone. But enough of that... Take the talisman with pride and walk the path of your chosen goddess," Naveh stated.

Dante did as he was told, gasping at the cold echo of his own power resonating through the talisman into his body. He felt it drawing in his lifeforce and focusing it before pushing his own power back into his body.

"What does this talisman do? I mean, I know Lapis Lazuli protects the mind and such..."

Naveh smiled. "It will focus your power and enhance your magic like all talismans, but in addition to that, your specific talisman will protect your soul from Underworld magic, help bridge the gap between you and the souls you touch, and enhance your empathetic powers as a necromancer and healer. Oh, and as you get more skilled, you can add spells or store powers into it. That will take some time though. Now let's go. I want you to find your chosen weapons before the day is out."

Gifts of War
and Life

Naveh did not expect much from Dante when it came to combat. The boy just oozed a cerebral edge, not a martial one. Still, he did well in some athletic endeavors. He may not have been able to run fast or knew how to throw a punch, but he could hit hard and had a fantastic pain tolerance and a good focus. He was clumsy, though awkward, and clearly was not comfortable with any of their work there.

There was also the fact that, due to his mortal blood, he lacked the physical advantages that even a drop of immortal blood gave to you. The boy would never be a powerhouse in combat, at least outside of magic, and likely even with magic. He was more a healer, a philosopher, than anything else, which sadly would translate into more danger in their dangerous era.

It made Naveh want to help the boy all the more. He was tired of so many people perishing due to the evils and hate of the bitter, bored immortals.

"Dante, we are going to try seeing what weapon goes for you." Naveh flared his magic. From a rune on his hand came a spear, a long bronze spear that oozed heat and his own rust-colored magic. "This is my personal weapon, I made it myself. It has the blessing of Hephaestus in my blood imbued into it, granting power over fire and heat in general. Let's see what weapon is your match." He turned toward the wall. "Christopher, come here please."

The Training Hall was massive, a circular room in the backyard of Hecate's temple, expanded with magic to be a massive coliseum made of obsidian-colored stone. In the center was a plain of dirt and dried blood, likely from previous games or training sessions. Dante felt rather unsafe, hating violence of any kind, but he knew he had no real choice but to be there.

At Naveh's command, someone came from one of the open arches on the sides of the walls. They were carrying a rack of weapons, all shiny and radiating enchantments. It was a boy, flickering with light, and he was adorable. Short with a nice angular face and soft-looking hair, however, he was hard to look at. He looked almost faded.

As if he was dead, Dante thought, his heart breaking for the boy before him. *Who would have killed a child?* And like that, his hatred of violence tripled in strength.

Christopher hurried over, smiling at them. "I brought everything. I knew you'd be calling me, Naveh." The boy's voice had an effeminate edge to it, light and almost airy, but very sweet. A closer look revealed a strong but soft, athletic frame, visible behind a grey toga, alongside a bloody swath across his throat.

Heart aching, Dante reached out and grabbed the spirit's hand in a rather impulsive move, his other hand moving instinctively to his new talisman. Cold magic surged through him, and he managed to actually connect with Christopher's faux skin.

With wide eyes, Christopher looked at him. "You're the first person to touch me in six months." His tone shifted, turning scratchy and pained, but also as joyous as humanly possible. "How did you do that?"

Naveh rolled his eyes at them both. "The talisman he is wearing enables and strengthens his magic, which is tied to necromancy. I am no expert but I do know that the first step of that sort of magic is touch. Now, if you two are done, let's get started. Dante, grab a weapon."

Christopher's brow furrowed. "Can I stay and watch?"

"Sure. Just don't get in the way or laugh too much," Naveh said.

What happened next was an embarrassing display of ineptitude that lasted over thirty minutes. No weapon seemed to fit Dante in any way. He had little coordination, less skill, and no confidence to even fake it. He felt horrible, but Naveh did not give up. Eventually, he thrust a silver bow and quiver into Dante's hand, pointing to a set of targets that lined the walls.

Dante, desperate to be good at something, put all of his focus into his attempt, and actually hit the damn target. It was off-centered, barely touching the target, but hey it was something.

"Hey, look, I am not a total failure!" Dante exclaimed.

Naveh laughed, as did Alex, while Christopher clapped happily. "Very good. Very, very good. Archery is your focus, but we should also work on your swordplay. That will likely take longer, but we will be working mostly with hand-to-hand and archery."

"Thanks, Naveh," Dante smiled.

The man waved away his thanks. "Just doing my job... Keep the bow, it's enchanted to be durable and channel your magic in times of need. You are not skilled enough to use it for much for now, but eventually, you should be able to use it for something."

Christopher hurried over, clapping happily. "That was awesome!"

It was hard for Dante to hide his blush, but Christopher was handsome and he was being complimented. "Thank you, but I barely hit the target," he said.

"When I tried, it took me forever to find a weapon. I ended up being good with a quarterstaff, or at least, not terrible," Christopher said.

Dante frowned, not asking what he wanted to ask, shifting his thoughts outward. "What was your magical focus?"

"Oh, animal enchantment." Christopher beamed.

A soft snort drew Dante's attention to the knowing eyes of Naveh. "You are on magic restriction today, so you have off until you have to work in the Healing Wing. Alex, why don't you hang with him? Should keep him out of trouble."

"Sure!" Both Dante and Christopher said, sharing looks of excitement.

"Bah, go have fun, you two," Naveh said, looking at Alex. "Three," he amended, "I have a lot of work to catch up on. Dante, be back here every evening at six. We will work for a few hours, give you time to rest and recover and study, then you will work with and for Lenore at the Healing Wing. Now, off with you."

"Nah, I think I am going to let the kiddos have their fun," Alex said. "See you later, Dante." And then he vanished in a swirl of mist.

As Alex walked away, Christopher got closer to Dante. "Want to see something cool?"

"Sure."

"Follow me."

And so Dante did, down through the door he first came in, and through several halls, until they reached the outside again. The smell of hey and dog hit him immediately, followed by barks and ups and other such noises. He then saw it... a den of dogs all playing in what looked like a barn.

Dante's brow rose. "Why the dogs?"

Christopher smiled. "Grandma Hecate's sacred animals are dogs, polecats, and frogs. She has all in her temple. Dogs are her favorite though, and my mom used to raise them for her in California. That was what I was going to do before I ... died." He choked up a little, as anyone who just died would have.

Dante grabbed his arm again, trying to convey warmth and light and comfort. "Do you want to talk about it?"

Christopher sighed. "The invasion yesterday wasn't the first. My family was pretty minor; we lived in a temple in California. We just raised her dogs; we have since the gods first returned. There was an attack by a sea monster. You see, the war right now is between the Ocean gods and the rest. The Seas are so polluted from the before times, and no one is helping the Ocean gods, who are being tainted and poisoned by the waters now... Same with all Freshwater beings. They are pissed. The Earthen gods are looking to join. Anyway, they sent a sea monster that destroyed our home and a host of warriors, children of the Waters. One found me, and he..." Christopher struggled to finish, his hand moving toward his throat, shivering.

Dante pulled him into a hug, uttering a spell before he could stop himself fully.

I give it now to thee, a gift of deepest empathy. I take your struggle, your pain. In solitude we stand, peace you gain.

Silver light enveloped them both, and something odd happened. A fraction of pain flowed from Christopher's ghostly form and into his own soul. He let out a long sigh, matching Dante's groan. The ghost's form seemed to relax, easing itself into his loving embrace.

"Thank you," Christopher said as they pulled apart. He smiled and cried a little, and then he rubbed his face. "I didn't bring you here to talk about my death and cry. I wanted to show you something... Come with me." He led Dante into the kennel proper, where he dropped to his knees. "I came back!" he said, arms wide. The dogs rushed him, barking and bunting him, their bodies actually making contact, likely from Hecate's blessing. "One day, you might get one as a familiar. I thought you might like to see them now."

Dante smiled and nodded. "Maybe..." He too fell to his knees, happy and eager, even if he wasn't a dog person. They scared him; they were loud and slobbery and could bite, but he wanted to soothe Christopher, so it was a sacrifice he was all too willing to make.

Hecate had been drawn in by the spell used to create Dante's necromantic talisman. How could it not, what with it being crafted from Hell Hound bones? She watched him fail at combat, chuckling a little at his eager attempts and discomfort. However, as a mother, she could not help but coo at his reaction to her grandson Christopher. There was an instant attraction, which was nice but also a deep lack of judgment that she profoundly appreciated.

Following them to the kennels, her heart ached at the memory of Christopher's death. He was so young, a mere fourteen, the same age as Dante in fact. What really caught her attention was what happened after he shared his death with Dante.

I give it now to thee, a gift of deepest empathy. I take your struggle, your pain. In solitude we stand, peace you gain.

Though simple and weak, the spell was something she never saw coming. A blending of necromancy and healing. A profound offering of empathy and trust. A spell that required a two-way street: empathy from Dante, and real trust from Christopher. It was simply beautiful.

"The boy is something else, isn't he?" Alex said as he appeared next to her, cloaking his form expertly on the astral plane she was watching from.

"Yes, he is. Not many would even choose to touch the dead, let alone feel enough empathy as to take in their pain and have enough empathy to make that magic a reality." She pondered. "I wonder if they are bonded. I saw no destiny for Dante..." She looked closer, focusing into the boy's soul, seeing past his recent oath to Styx to serve her, and saw he had no soulmate. He was bound to no one. "No, he is free of any links. Hmmm, the beginnings of puppy love I presume."

Alex shrugged. "Whatever it is, I hope it will be good for him. Neither boy has had it easy, and if nothing else, they will be good friends."

"Yes... that would be nice. My grandson needs more friends; he is not fitting in well with the other ghosts present. He is so young and sometimes forgets he is dead." Hecate resisted the urge to cry, her heart aching at the notion. "Do you think Dante would like a familiar?"

"Perhaps he will, I am not sure. As deeply as I care for him, which is more than I ought to, he and I have only known each other a week. I cannot say I know him that well..."

Hecate nodded. "I see... Well, hopefully, he does in fact want one. I would happily give it my blessing. But until then, let us leave these sweet boys to their play date."

And like that, both goddess and ghost vanished, leaving behind no trace they were ever present, to begin with.

The Great Libraries

"Finally!" Dante beamed as Lenore's hands passed over him, glowing a soft, velvet.

It had been a busy three days of healing. He would work out with Naveh and practice his archery, practice his typical magical-like fire-starting and telekinesis with Alex, work with Lenore by cleaning the hall or the patients, study the words he wrote from the beginners magic book from the Inheritance Library, or hang out with Christopher in the kennel. He barely cast any magic, only the weakest and the most basic of the craft, in a desperate attempt to not further the damage to his soul but to keep his new skills fresh. It was hard to restrain himself now that he did not need to use a talisman to draw power from the air. He could do it on his own, though it took far greater focus without the aid of Hecate's blessing.

Lenore rolled her eyes. "Yes, you are healed up, you can practice magic fully. You are lucky too. That spell you did to soothe Christopher's pain could have forced you into far more damage."

Dante grinned at her. "Sorry. But he was hurting, and I had to help."

"I know that. You have a healer's nature." She scowled at him playfully. "But you must temper it with caution, lest you overexert yourself. Now, since you are fully healed, and you have sworn your oaths, you can now enter the libraries for study. Remember, you can only take out five books at once, and only beginner books. The rest are spelled to prevent you access, painfully, so do not press your luck. Now go. Enjoy yourself. Oh, and if I were you, I'd go into the Underworld door. You already have a teacher for all of your affinities, as well as basic magic, with Alex being your guide. Underworld magic will be something you must learn on your own, at least until you impress Lady Hecate enough to get you access to a better teacher."

Dante nodded and rushed away, happy to be finally in his full element, one of study and knowledge and power. It was where he was meant to be and it was drawing out his full self, every part of him he normally kept in check. Excitement, happiness, and childlike wonder. Pieces of his soul he never let free.

Reaching the place where his affinities had been tested, he quickly found himself between the doors of the Underworld and Earth. They pulled on him, mentally and magically. Taking a deep breath, he turned to the Underworld door and hurried inside. Instantly he felt darkness flood his soul. It tasted like Alex and Christopher's auras, only magnified a hundredfold, the pure essence of the Underworld.

Inside, there were thousands of books on hundreds of shelves, all different colors and radiating potent powers. There were desks with a handful of priests and ghosts sitting by. The ghosts were almost solid, which startled him.

"The magic here thins the veil. We are closer to the surface here." Alex said, making Dante jump and look at his infernal mentor, who was smirking deeply. "Now, let's get you started. Okay, kiddo? I studied this place while you slept. I found the books you want to start with. Come on." He led Dante away to a distant desk covered in a dozen books. "I checked them out. They will be left here for you while you study. You can take five out to your room to study, but you can leave the rest here. Now, the first book was written by Persephone herself, Queen of Hades and potent goddess. It was originally written for Hades and her priests, but this was added here when she realized that Hecate's children and priests would need it as well. It is a basic tome, addressing all aspects of your power. Necromancy, you should know, encompasses all of the Underworld magic. It was why Hecate was so impressed with you; you are able to use all Underworld magic in its entirety, which is also likely why you can divine as ghosts, at least some of us have a sense of time that differs so we can see the future and memories of the past linger in a way not unlike ghosts do."

Nodding, Dante grabbed the first book, a deep moss green colored tome. It was blank, but as he looked onto the yellowing pages, words started to appear. His mind was drawn in with familiar magnetic pressure, he could not look away.

> *Necromantic magic is simply the essence of drawing on Radiant energy filtered through the Underworld for the purpose of communing, controlling, and defeating the dead. By all means, it is by Force of Will that his magic finds its path, for a weak will would be burned out by those that mean to control, for to connect to the dead is to give it access to your power, just as you gain access to its power and knowledge and essence. That mutual connection is key, and so through a stronger will does one not find oneself drained of power and life and presence.*

> *To start, meditation is key. Imagine yourself a tree, with your roots digging deep into the Underworld, drawing frigid strength through your roots. Then, with that power and your will, connect through empathy and sympathy to those you wish to connect to. With all you are, extend your thoughts through the power and make the connection as you need it.*

Never forget yourself, lest you find yourself more dead than life. And never forget that no matter your will, the very act of connection grants power to the dead. You only ever have so much power to give, no matter your skill and strength.

This tome, written by my hand, will guide you through the various uses of our dark power and its effects on the body, soul, and mind, as well as on the world around its caster.

Pulling himself away, Dante turned to Alex. "This is intense."

"Quite, but through it, you can make a true, rare difference. Are you willing to risk it?"

Dante frowned. "I think so..." He thought of Christopher, unwillingly, and so a question burned in his chest. *Can ghosts age?*

Alex smiled. "Through a necromancer, yes. That is a piece of knowledge I learned through Aphrodite actually. Connecting life to death helps them absorb mental change, and grow... It is through a weaker process that I learned to make my death mark. Without it, you'd see a bloody hole on my stomach."

Dante shivered. "That is... terrifying."

"I imagine it is... Why do you ask? It isn't for Christopher, is it?"

Dante's cheeks burned. "Maybe it is. He's nice and sweet and... he deserves better than to be fourteen forever. I want to help him live, even if he's dead."

"A noble task, but one with great risk. You must never forget, as the tome states, that connecting like that to a dead being, no matter how pure, has its risks. He could siphon your strength too much, weakening you without intention... He could kill you, make you the living dead, drive you to madness by taking your mental strength... Please, be careful, kiddo."

Fear fluttered through Dante's chest. "I will keep that in mind... but to be honest, I aim to help you too."

Alex looked stunned. "Me?"

"I know we just met, but I really want to hug you. I know your son was a prick but you deserve better... and you've been so kind. So, yeah."

Tears fell down Alex's face, and he radiated a sense of love so strong it made him glow neon grey. "You are a really good kid, you know that right?"

"I guess so, but it's really nice to hear." Dante hated that he choked up, but he did. "Um... let's get back to the book. I really want to see what I can do with this new magic!"

He never noticed the soft eyes of Hecate watching from the shadows.

"Maybe he could be what I needed..." Hecate sighed, her voice aching as she watched the boy study. "He cares for even the dead, which is rare, necromantic talent or not. With a finger in the magic of each realm, drawing on them all for strength, he could easily be what I need... He could connect to the gods of all... He could be my ambassador, just as I envisioned."

Her mind turned to the first day she saw him, and the potential she sensed. Intelligence, compassion, a natural survivor, defiant and respectful, independent... The boy was a perfect mixture born of a hard life rather than bloodline or destiny. Hecate saw only the tiniest glimmer of a future, one that radiated peace and strife in equal measure, and she knew it might be all she needed to end this war.

She was an ambassador to all of the gods, but she needed a mortal aid. Mortals were easily changing and adaptable, and they saw things beyond tradition. The boy, with his strong will and natural independence, could see patterns the gods just couldn't, the demigods and blessed beings couldn't. He was free from those biases, and that made him perfect.

Lenore was a great priestess, but she was immersed too deeply in the magical world, coming from an old blessed bloodline of witches. Naveh had his own goals and was using her more than seeking to save others. The others were imperfect in their own ways.

Dante was potentially perfect; he was just what they needed... to help end the war and stop it from escalating. She only needed him to gain power, to gain skill, to open his eyes to the world and see it for what it really was... and soon before it was far too late. If not, she might intervene before she'd wanted to, before he was ready, mighty, and able to handle the egotistical monsters that were the other gods...

Blessed Darkness, Cursed Light

*J*ust as Persephone's tome said, Dante imagined himself as a mighty tree—a Rowan since it was powerful protective magic—and drank deep of the Underworld's cold potency. Immediately he noticed a difference between doing this and drinking of the free-floating, radiant energy present in the air. It was colder, darker, and deader. Radiant energy was pure and open to change, but this was stagnant and rigid. Death was universal, and when you died you stayed unchanged unless you were reborn. So really, it made sense.

Opening his eyes, Dante saw a thin aura of shadow mist over his body. It drank in the silvery light of the sconces, rendering the air colder and dimmer. It followed his hand as he moved it, like an afterimage, creating a trail of regular mist as he moved, and it sucked up the heat around him. His talisman was glistening, its protective magics soothing the cold ache the Underworld magic ought to have had, or so his instinct told him.

Alex, leaning down, smiled at him with paternal love. "You okay, kid?"

"I think so... yeah." Reaching out, Dante grabbed Alex's hand, the magic linking them together. "See, good!"

Alex felt odd, though less real than when he hugged Christopher, almost like hugging a bunch of cold water than a solid figure, but it was progress. Still, he wondered why there was a difference... Standing slowly, he imagined the power draining back into the earth and all the way to the Underworld, with a soft thank you as he did so.

"Great. Great job, kiddo."

Dante beamed. "I do try... And to think that someday that will be not just automatic but easy!"

"I wouldn't go so far as to say easy—no magic really is—but easier."

Dante shrugged. "Fair enough." Then he stumbled, a wave of exhaustion hitting him. "Damn! I'm still mortal, still weak, no matter my sensitivity." He sat down, holding his head in his hand. "I have no excess radiant energy stored in my cells to feed my magic. I am still using my lifeforce, which is not yet expanded from the practice of magic. Ugh... "

Alex laughed. "Consider that a lesson in hubris, kiddo. You have limits. Never forget that, lest you lose your life."

"Yeah, trust me. The world will never let me forget that..."

Memories unbidden flooded his mind, mocking comments about his plainness, his weight, his mortality, his lack of stamina and divinity. His siblings, all athletic, never really had to endure it as much, but he had. He took after his mother far more than the others, but even she had been more athletic than he. He had always been a scholar, which was not as cool in these warring days, where being a warrior was the way to be seen as fantastic. Serving the gods on the front lines, fighting the good fight and all that...

It made him wretch but also burned through a wound in his soul that would likely never fade. A wound born of the cruelty of humanity and children, who were never as innocent as adults seemed to think. Of course, adults had allowed the cruelty so...

It was years ago, you are now a priest in training to the goddess you admire most. You are a witch, you have friends that you may very well love one day... That is the past, this is the future. Times change, times move on and so much you.

Shaking off the weight of years gone by, he stood. "I can't practice that again, not at the moment. I need rest and time... but I can read some more about the Underworld, its hierarchy, the rules of summoning, how I can utilize my powers... "

Alex smiled. "Yes, yes, you can and you ought to."

And so, turning back to the book written by Persephone, Dante began to read.

The book wove a brilliant tale, of the arranged marriage of Persephone to Hades, how they came to love each other, and how Persephone had been the only ancient queen to hold equal power with her husband. She held full sway over the Underworld and was the only god or goddess of her generation to rival the power of her father's generation, of the first generation of Olympians.

It told of Hecate's service to the gods during the Titan war, how she was granted full sway over all of the realms as a reward. He smiled when he read of how she aided Demeter in finding Persephone, and how she was made Persephone's servant. He cheered when he read how Hecate was granted the position of ambassador after Ragnarok, serving no god or goddess but being considered a servant to the World itself, while retaining the respect and favor of the Underworld as magic worked best on the fringe, on the crossroads and shadowed steps.

Melione, Megara, Zaggerus, Thanatos, Lethe, Styx, Charon, and countless others were given their own stories, though they paled in comparison to the other gods. Morpheus and Hypnos were given two lines each, the God of Dreams and Sleep respectively, despite their vast powers. Each was considered a powerful ally, soldier, and leader in their spheres, but they all served Persephone and Hades.

Most interesting, however, was that their powers showed what he could do with his necromantic powers. With enough training and with proper effort, he would hold influence over Dreams and Sleep, Ghosts and the Dead, Forgetfulness and Remembrance, Divination of the past and memories and auras, Judgement and Forgiveness, Curses and Oaths, Riches and the Preservation of Life. These were the powers of the Underworld. These were the powers he would one day hold to.

Amazed, he turned to a stunned Alex. "I had no idea that the Underworld had such spheres of influence!"

"Nor did I. Nor did I."

Hecate wanted to cackle, watching the boys read her old friend's mystical tome. So many doubted the magic of the Underworld, never realizing its potential and power beyond messing with the dead. The Underworld held great sway on the world order, the very essence of life required death to keep it going, to help recycle the old into new, cleaner energy! There was a reason Persephone, bearer of the essence of life itself, was the Queen of the Underworld!

"Always so much fun to see this sight; a pity it is a so rare one." Giggling to herself, feeling her maiden essence taking hold, Hecate felt the urge to skip around the boy mockingly, but she held fast to the much more mature Mother and Crone to stifle that urge. "It wouldn't do to be seen in such a state, not by such a recent follower." Breathing out the urge to be silly, she stood tall. "The boy can really only do the most basic of magic. But tapping into Underworld magic even once awakens one's capacity to have mystical dreams, and with the war and massive deaths going on, the boy will be for a really terrible ordeal..." Sighing, she flicked her fingers at one of the other books, written by a priest of Morpheus. It fluttered open, and the boys jumped. "There, duty is done."

Dante moved to the page. "What the hell?" His eyes widened. "Holy Hecate! Alex, it says here that by tapping into Underworld magic, my mind is automatically opened to the currents of the dream world. Astral projection, a facet of that power, can begin to happen naturally. My mind and soul can be drawn to massive events, scenes of great turmoil, and explosions of magic. People, gods mostly, can summon me! However, since I am mortal and lack the spiritual flexibility that those of divine or blessed blood have, it will be dangerous to my brain and body. I could go mad, have a cerebral hemorrhage or a stroke... It could kill me or damage my soul!"

Alex grabbed onto him, never realizing that he was actually making contact despite the lack of Underworld power emanating from the boy. "We need to get you some protection! What about your talisman? It is supposed to keep you safe from harm caused by the Underworld."

"It says that talismans of Underworld ties can and do help, but it is best that I do not astral-project without casting protective spells—ritualistic magics. It also says that I am at risk of being possessed... but if I am summoned, then the summoner's magic is automatically protecting me. Actually, it says they cannot cast aside their protection at all, even the most powerful of the gods." Dante flipped through the pages. "It says there are spells that one can cast, runes etched onto the skin, that can help protect the body and mind. We can have them cast now, but it is beyond my skill. We will need help, lest my new power destroys my mind!"

Grabbing the book, Dante fled the library with Alex at his heels, never seeing Hecate's pleased smile.

"Damn, I'm good. Lenore can cast those runes, as could Naveh, both have the power and skill."

Nevah pressed his thumb into Dante's spine, at the very top. The boy hissed as his magic, which was naturally hot, burned him. "Stop being a baby. You asked for this."

"Still hurts, but thanks. I wish someone would have warned me that my powers could harm me so much."

"There is a reason magic is not used by all. It always has a cost—all magic. Diviners can be lost, their minds overloaded by the past or stretched too thin by the streams of time. Healers can be overtaken by their patient's pain. Enchanters can lose their essence to their creations, or infuse too much of themselves within them. Those wielding the powers of shape-shifting—a sea power—can be stuck in their animal forms, overruled by primal instinct. Even botanical magics can hold danger, your lifeforce consumed by the plants you raise. Magic is not a game, it is work, it is effort, and it is dangerous. Why should Underworld magic, ruled and embodied by some of the greatest of the gods, be any exception?"

Dante raised a hand, giving Naveh an okay sign. "I guessed as much when I read about my lifeforce being the cost of using pure magic through pure Radiant energy, and the cost being death. I literally died and damaged my soul. I know it comes at a cost, but this one was… far more than I realized. I should have been warned."

Naveh sighed. "Yeah, you should have… It is not an excuse, but do not forget how rare Underworld magic is, especially with someone that can access so naturally the entire spectrum of that sphere of power. You are a rare kid. No one likely knew enough to tell you. Plus, most priests are demigods or legacies. We have spiritual flexibility, born of the gods being able to be in more than one place at a time. For us, it manifests as being able to divide our souls into our body and astral self. I can astral-project myself; it was too useful a skill to not learn. It, and mediumship, are the only Underworld magic I could manage. I struggle with empathy to do much." He shook his head, clearing it. "Anyway, like I said, we have that flexibility, but you don't, so people didn't think to tell you."

Dante's face couldn't be seen, but he knew he was pouting. "Will the tattoos help?"

"Yes and no. If you are meant to see something, are close enough to it, or it is big enough, you will be drawn out. A god can still take you out, even the weakest of them, or a strong mage. However, in any case, it will protect you, but it will still be very painful, and there is still a time limit. The good news is that, as magic amplifies and strengthens your mind, body, and soul, you will gain that flexibility among other things such as longer life, stronger lifeforce, better memory, superior body, and so on. Magic alters all it touches."

Putting the final touches on the magic, Naveh grabbed Dante's shoulders and admired his work for a minute. There was an arc of marks, starting at either shoulder and moving to the base of Dante's spine. It was good work, something to be proud of.

Clapping his hands, Naveh blasted magic through Dante who, to his credit, didn't scream but did let out a long groan as the magic seared and healed onto his skin, creating permanent marks. Letting go, he watched Dante sway then steady.

"Owe..."

Alex, who had been biting his illusionary nails, stepped forward. "Did it work?"

"Insulting me with your doubt? Of course, it worked. I cast those same runes on myself, you know!" Naveh pulled his shirt down, showing his marks. "I had an automaton write them, then cast them. Of course, I've been casting for longer than a week, unlike you..." He grabbed Dante's chin, looking into his eyes to make sure he was safe. "Get some rest, and you can go light on training tomorrow. The magic should have settled in by then."

Dante smiled at him. "Thanks, Naveh."

"No problem. You'll be surprised how many things you need to keep you safe as a magic user. We casters take a lot of risks to obtain power... Now go, I can sense Christopher waiting for you at my door."

Dante bowed low, then hurried over to the door and out it, where Christopher was indeed waiting, worried.

The boys chattered away at each other in an admittedly adorable manner as they walked away, with their ghost chaperone Alex shaking his head at them fondly as they hurried off.

Brighid's Light

Cleaning the Healing Wing was easy and methodical, giving Dante a lot of time to think and go over his spells and life in general. However, this day, one full week after becoming a priest in training to Hecate and gaining sensitivity to magic, two weeks after coming to New Olympus, he felt a familiar dread fall upon him. The hole in his soul had decided to reopen and unleash its misery once more.

He felt weary, a constant tiredness and apathy filled him. It wasn't boredom or a lack of passion; it was a lack of care, a numbness that sank into all aspects of his being. For as long as he could remember, it had been present, ebbing and flowing like the tides. Sometimes slamming into him like a tsunami, destroying his life. Other times it was deceptively gentle, wearing away at him bit by bit until he was raw.

He had no name for it, no one knew of it far as he was aware, but it was a constant in his life. He had hoped, absently, that magic would chase it away, but it seemed that magic was not as strong as this feeling. That hole in his soul seemed to numb more than his heart; it numbed his connection to magic. He could not feel the constant cool presence of the temple, taste the

BRIGHID'S LIGHT | 75

wintery magic of his talisman, or make any contact with his ghostly friends. His magic would not work as it should. He could barely touch the stream of radiant magic in the air, and in no way could he tap into the essence of the Underworld.

He said nothing to anyone, not even Alex or Christopher, or Naveh. He just pushed it off as having an off day, and they let it pass. No one knew that he stood in an abyss, one that had nearly taken his life more than once...

And so with this horrible numb agony in his entire being, he cleaned the Halls, close to tears and aching everywhere but his heart. In utter silence, for about twenty minutes, he cleaned and worked. It was only once he mopped the entire hall, reaching the far end where Lenore's office was, that something changed. Not within, but on the outside. It was a warmth, strong enough that it broke through his apathy for a moment, making him look up to see a familiar face.

"Brighid?"

The kindly healer beamed at him with her quirky smile. She was walking toward him with a swagger that most people just didn't carry with them. "Are you okay?" she asked, unbidden by anything he said or did.

Putting on a fake smile, Dante nodded. "Fine. Why do you ask?"

She pierced him with her eyes, their off-green burning through his deception. "I am a Priestess of Asclepius, from a long line of priests and priestesses on both sides of my family. I walk the path of Epione, the Goddess of Soothing pain. I help with surgeries and people passing into the Underworld and... I use my powers to help those like you, who suffer from depression."

Dante shivered, her words searing his apathy and filling him with the tiniest spark of hope. "What do you mean?"

"Healing isn't just for the body, it is about the mind and soul. Epione specializes in mental healing mostly, so through that path I can sense pain.

I sense your pain. The humans before the gods, blasphemous as they were, had a profound understanding of the mind. We took that knowledge and use it to care for our people. What I sense from you, though I didn't before, is depression. A chemical imbalance in the brain brought on by trauma and inheritance. Some people just have it..."

Her words slammed into Dante's soul like an angry Hercules. "There... I... Others have this?" He clenched his fist over his heart, and tears welled up in his eyes.

She nodded, her eyes softer. "I have it. It runs in families."

Dante bent over, feeling the rush of relief. His body shook as he lost his breath, the world swirling and magic prickled against his senses ever so slightly. "I am not alone..."

A warm hand placed itself on his head, magic seething from it and sinking into his essence, tempering not only the sudden rush of emotion but also the edge of the depression. He felt a measure of his true self surging forth, and with it a genuine smile.

"Just breathe, okay?"

He nodded. "Thank you... so much."

She shrugged. "Not a problem. It's what I do."

After a moment of silence, Dante asked, "Why are you here?"

"Oh, well, I work here too, cleaning and caring for patients at night. I like the quiet. I only worked a day shift when we first met due to the tragedy of the attack."

"I see... Well, there are no patients tonight, Lenore took care of them all, but you are free to help me clean."

She nodded, grabbing a rag and bucket. "Let's get to it."

Hours passed as they cleaned the entire wing from top to bottom. It was nice with them chatting, even if Brighid was not as much of a talker compared to him or Alex or Christopher. There was a warmth about her that made it easy to be around her, a silent strength that made him want to share his burdens with her. She was an eager ear too, listening kindly and giving advice or just listening to him talk.

She shared a lot about her life, how her father was a mind healer and her mother a physical healer. How she was actually not a legacy of any kind but was from a family of healers from before the gods returned, and so she was blessed by Asclepius and Epione, even if there were no physicians in her family, just nurses and counselors. Or how she, despite being a healer, excelled at combat magic with a focus on swordplay and hand-to-hand combat and botany, having been trained in both after begging her friends in Hecate's temple. She was a full-blown witch in addition to the blessing Asclepius and Epione gave their followers.

Speaking of her blessing, it was incredible. It gave her the power to sense, absorb and disperse pain without a spell. She could speed up healing, mute infections, and invoke cleanliness, since she also studied the path of Hygeia, Goddess of Good Health and Hygiene, the daughter of Epione and Asclepius. She was a moderately powerful priestess, mostly working in the hospital, with a general focus on pain mediation, though she had other talents. She was young too, only sixteen years old.

And so, naturally, they became fast friends.

"There are spells that can help with depression," she said after a while, once they finished up. "I use them. They are meditation prayers to Epione. The previous generation would use medication. The prayer spell works best for short-term release. It sort of takes the edge off, but it won't cure. It helps you function and gives you back your sensitivity to magic. For the long term, you need a potion, I will help you with that. I have been making it for the last four years to take the edge off."

"Thank you."

She shrugged again; she did that a lot. "No one should have to suffer through this. It is utter hell... Now, for the prayer spell, remember to be respectful. You are invoking a goddess. Epoine used to be human, so she tends to be more empathetic toward this sort of thing..."

A Painful Promise

Closing his eyes in front of his desk, armed with poppies, Dante drew on radiant energy with his hand. Closing his eyes, he chanted the first nonrhyming spell he had ever attempted. It was a prayer spell, taught to him by Brighid, in a desperate attempt to stem the tide of his depression. He had to focus hard and truly mean the prayer.

"Lady Epione, Goddess of Soothing Pain. I offer to you this gift of magic and poppies, which soothes the wounds of the flesh. With these offerings, please render from me the raw edge of the sharp depression smothering my soul. Give me the chance—the means—to walk light and not endless shadow." Gathering the energy into his palm, he blew on the magic just as he opened his eyes. In an instant, the magic changed from the silver of the moon to the warm orange of a sunset, swirling around the offering.

The poppies vanished in a ripple of magic—his offering was accepted—before the new orange magic shot back at him, sinking into his temples. Warmth and magic radiated through him, and he felt a spurt of emotion and light come back as the magic burned away the darkness of his cloying depression.

He never expected the loving touch of a mother echoing in his mind, nor a soft sweet sight of a woman filling the air. There was no one there, but Epione felt his pain and gave him what he asked for. He bowed low, genuine appreciation in his heart.

"I will grant you a greater offering another time when I have the means. Thank you so much," Dante said, through the tears now cascading down his face.

After a few minutes, he wiped the tears away and moved to his bed, closing his eyes to sleep, only to instantly feel sheer weightlessness overtake him. Eyes wrenching open, he realized he was floating. Turning, he saw himself lying in bed, blood dripping from his eyes, his skin paler than normal.

"Great. Who is summoning me now?" Dante uttered.

"That would be me," a voice answered.

Dante would have jumped if he could. Turning, he saw a woman with brown and black hair looking at him, dressed in a priestess's uniform. Only she radiated far greater power than any priestess, except maybe Lenore who felt godlike.

The voice was familiar. He had just heard it sigh a moment ago. "Epione?"

"Yes, and you must see something." She vanished in a swirl of wind that wrapped around him and carried him off and away, far into the air, through the temple and into the sky, across the city of New Olympus. Dante half expected her to take him away out of the city and to a bloody scene, but they stopped on the north end of the city, directly opposite where he had stayed two weeks ago.

"Why here?" he asked.

The goddess's voice echoed in his head and heart. "You offered a greater offering when I soothed your soul. Serve me in this, and your debt will be fulfilled in full. You will never need to offer me anything more, and I will offer my full aid to you one time in healing another."

Dante shivered, real fear entering his soul. "What could I do that would help you? I am so new to the craft."

She answered by sending him closer to the city—closer and closer until he saw a familiar face... several familiar faces. His fear exploded within him, as well as hate and greater sadness than his depression was capable of.

"What are they doing here?" Dante asked. "You cannot expect me to help them, not after what they did to me."

Again he was not answered with words but action, and so he was sent closer and closer until he was right next to the people who invoked such strong misery. The only people who could... His mortal family...

Front and center was his father, who had aged twenty years in the two since he last saw him. The man was bronze-skinned with black hair now peppered with white. He had a large bulbous nose and an air of anger about him. He used to be handsome, but a hard life in the sun and so much hate burned that away. However, what drew Dante most was the angry, sharp, intelligent near-black eyes. They looked nothing alike, and yet their minds were so similar that it hurt. Sometimes he opened his own mouth and heard his father's voice come out.

Next to his father was his blonde wife, Anne, short and ugly with not a single good feature. She wasn't even smart; he had no idea how or why his father got with her. She was utterly beneath him, and yet she held the power in their relationship. She had used that power to get his father, Erik, to abandon his children emotionally and Dante physically.

Behind them were Rose and Markus, his siblings. Rose was his mother's thinner, more athletic double. She wasn't as smart as he was, but she was social and athletic as any demigod. Markus was dull as a match, looking like their maternal grandfather almost exclusively, what with his tanned skin and dopey smile.

He heard his father speaking to Anne, his tone soft and pained. "What are we going to do? This place only employs legacies or demigods, those born to Hephaestus line." His father was a builder and damn good at it, but biases were biases. "We can't feed ourselves for much longer, let alone the kids."

Anne sighed. "I know..." For once she seemed sad for someone other than her or her kids, who were all adults and thus apparently free of the situation they were in.

Shaking, Dante sighed. "They lived in Bolivar too. They must be some of the survivors... I forgot they lived so close. I never saw them." And then he looked up. "Do you know their evils? He beat and berated me for years, hating me and hurting me and my siblings. She inspired his cruelty and violence. She hated us for taking from her kids by existence, calling us ugly and worthless and stupid..."

The voice of the goddess echoed in his head. "They beseeched me for salvation, not with their words but the pain in their hearts. I am the Goddess of Soothing Pain—all pain when I can help it—and this is a pain I can help, through you and your deeds. You are in a position of power now, and through that, you can do greater good beyond your magic. You are a healer... Can you stand looking at them, knowing they are in agony, close to starvation and possibly death? Even your siblings, who committed no crime toward you?"

"My father and Anne deserve death, but they don't... and my siblings need protection and parental guidance..." Dante groaned and said the words that filled his soul with greater anguish still. "I will figure something out..."

And with finality, he flew back to his body at blinding speeds, crashing through the temple, only to fall into his skin and finally into sleep. The magic of Epione, sweet and soft, lulled him away from the pain he ought to have been feeling and pushed him fully into Morpheus' realm. His last thought before he went to bed, other than thinking about his unfortunate promise and the vile people he shared blood with, was rather simple. *I hope I don't get blood on my bed...*

Lenore's Lessons

"And by drawing on the Earth, the majesty of Gaia, as is your mortal birthright, you can use it to soothe any wound, heal any injury and push away any infection," Lenore said, her tone intentionally wise and magnanimous. The boy looked dreary, she sensed his depression was holding fast to his soul and so she put in more effort to capture his intelligence. "The Power of Gaia can be used for many other things, like increasing strength, creating protective barriers, dowsing for others, controlling plant life, connecting with animals, and so on. Your connection to the Underworld is oddly stronger than your ties to the Earth, or so I've noticed. So you may find some struggle with Gaia's power. Healing is going to be your major earthbound magic, and so that is what we will focus on."

Dante nodded, fingering his talisman. "Will this interfere?"

"No, it should not. Hellhounds are creatures of the Earth and Underworld, and Silver is a universal material. All should be well." She leaned down. "What is wrong? Beyond your depression, which we've discussed, I sense something else is wrong with you. It is robbing your focus."

Sighing, Dante looked up to her and let out his woes in one long-winded spiel of pain, misery, and confusion. Her heart broke for him.

"A goddess is all, but forcing you to aid your abusive family in return for the magic needed to manage through your depression, is cruel but not unexpected," Lenore said.

"Yeah, I thought so too... but I cannot figure out how to help. I have so little influence, even if I know exactly how I'd help them."

That caught Lenore's attention. "How would you help them?" she asked.

"I'd get my father a job under a Legacy of Hephaestus. My father may be mad and evil and uncaring but he is a damn good builder and leader. Having a job, income, and so on would fulfill all of the requirements for my promise to Epione."

"I see... Well, in that case, I can help. I have connections to many people. I will speak to Naveh and see if we can get one of his cousins to help with this. However, you must confront your father and your past. Do not let it define you, hold sway over you, or you will never find peace."

Pure hate filled Dante's eyes, muddled only by fear. "I— Please don't— Fine!" He slumped down, no longer expressing his pain, masking it entirely under a false veil of apathy.

Lenore sighed. "Now, let us work on drawing Gaia's power. Prepare yourself for the surge of physical strength. Never forget the most potent wielder of Gaia's physical power, Anteus, who could not be harmed or killed so long as he was touching the earth. He, a mere giant, fought Hercules himself, a demigod and legacy of Zeus, legacy of Poseidon, and inheritor of Hera's forced blessing.

Tapping into this power is not unlike Underworld magic. Imagining yourself as a tree is key, but this time, draw from the surface and do not let your roots dig so deep. Draw from the Earth mother, not the Underworld. Oh, I should also mention that, whereas the Underworld holds mental power,

Gaia's inherent power is physical. So, even if you are not using it for anything, your healing and physical powers will drastically increase."

Dante nodded, interest seeping back into his eyes, his passion for magic unable to be entirely blocked by his pain and apathy.

Erik had no idea why he had been summoned by the High Priestess of Hecate's temple. He knew none of his brood held any ties to magic. They were too simple-minded for the craft, if he was being honest with himself. He too was far too angry for magic; he had been tested as a child for it, as so many were. So, without any idea of why, he brought his family forth through the Silver and Gold gates of the Second and First District to the Temple of Hecate.

He stopped outside, just as he was ordered, seeing three people standing tall in front of the building. Two were mystery people, but the last was so familiar that it made his chest ache.

"Dante?" he asked, seeing his son bearing an aura of power that told of magic and mystery.

Dante, his eldest son and second born sighed. "Yes, dad... It's me." Turning, he gestured to the two people; a tall black woman with strong muscles and curly black hair, and a tall light-skinned man with a scruffy red beard. Both were scowling at him, hatefully. "This is Lenore, Head High Priestess of the Temple, and Naveh, High Priest of Construction for Hecate's temple. They are my mentors."

His son's tone was cold but oddly not hateful. It was as if he had been drained of all emotion, leaving behind nothing but deficiency and apathy. It enraged Erik, his eyes narrowing at what he perceived to be disrespectful.

He wasn't stupid though; expressing anger at his son in front of two powerful priests would not be wise.

And so he put on a false smile. "It is an honor to meet you."

"Not really," Naveh said. "We know the kind of man you are. Your son shared his memories with us."

Erik whipped to his son, who stared back defiantly. "Consequences, Erik..."

Stepping forward, the mortal father was stopped by a pulse of cold energy coming from the woman Lenore.

"Do not try it! I will rend your soul from your flesh!" she said, her tone almost bored.

Shaking with hate, Erik settled for glaring at his son. "He always did exaggerate. A dramatic child that—"

"Do you think I am a fool?" Lenore said, her words searing his skin, even though she did not raise her voice. "I am a master of most magics. Reading his memories was effortless. You cannot modify them with his current skill level. I know you, Erik. Your evil, your cruelty... and so it is with great pride in Dante that I make this offer, or rather Naveh makes this offer."

Naveh stepped forward. "My uncle works for the Temple of Hephaestus, building and repairing buildings and the walls. He is willing to employ you. Make your choice, you only get it once."

Hating everyone before him, Eric opened his mouth to rage, only to see Anne's glare. He deflated. "Fine. I accept."

"Good. Oh, and you should know, this was Dante's idea, all so his brother and sister do not starve." Naveh waved his hand, and a red swirl of light appeared. When it faded, there was a paper fluttering toward him. Erik grabbed it. "That is the instructions to where you will meet to get started. Now, begone with you!"

With that, the three priests left, leaving Erik raw, confused, and very, very grateful...

Hecate hated herself; her deal with Epione was a cruel one. Getting Dante to make a hard choice for the greater good of others, even at the cost of his own happiness... That was a test and one that she needed to see if the boy was to be her Ambassador. His ability to be objective was a vital one.

Watching from the shadows, she walked closer to Dante, eager to pay him back for this painful deed, and she heard him speaking to Naveh.

"Even your siblings seemed to hate you. I saw them glaring at you... Why?"

Dante shrugged. "We never loved each other. My family pitted us against each other far too often, but the biggest part is that they are loyal to Erik and I turned against him my whole life. I never put up with his cruelty. I knew it was wrong and I fought back. They resented that..."

Hecate cringed more at those words. "I really need to do something nice for the boy..."

Dante continued, "My father set my entire family against me, saying my mother cheated and conceived me. He used that to justify the abuse and hate. Nothing I did was right. I think my siblings bought into that on some level, if nothing else it created some space between us."

Lenore reached out, her cool hands brushing Dante's cheek. "You did well. So few would have helped their abusers."

"I wasn't helping him, I was helping them. They may not be people I love, but my siblings do not deserve starvation. They are basically strangers, and I would have done that service for any stranger."

And with that simple expression of altruism, Hecate knew that the boy was exactly what she was looking for.

She had found her ambassador!

Now, if only the gods would wait long enough for him to mature and grow in magic...

Infernal Love

The arms of Christopher, ephemeral and ghostly, wrapped around a weary Dante, impressing on him a sense of love and peace that he rarely found elsewhere. Alex's arms, equally false, did the same. They held him for a while in his room, doing their best to soak up his despair. The wound in his soul opened via seeing his monstrous father once more. The reminder that the man that should have been his most arduous protector hated him so deeply was something that left a scar on the soul.

Christopher leaned in, ever grateful for his friend's Underworld magic, and placed a gentle kiss on his cheek. "How are you feeling?" he asked, soft and sweet and with only the purest of intent.

His friend, who was not crying but looked deader than Christopher literally was, sighed. "Better, oddly, but not great. It wasn't just seeing him that hurt, it was the reminder that he hates me so much, and no matter how much I hate him I can't seem to throw away the urge to help and impress him. I wanted to chat with him, brag to him, with him. He wasn't always evil; he could be funny, kind, and sweet. He was charming and smart at times...

He was nurturing even. It made it that much harder to tear myself away two years ago when I had the choice to enter foster care."

"I was watching in my less visible form, and his aura was confused and ridden with insecurities. He was not a good man." Alex sighed. "That is not on you, he made his choices."

Dante nodded. "I know, but it doesn't erase the feelings of pain."

"I imagine it does not... So, what now?"

"I am not sure. I just want to never see him or them again, not if I can control it. I made sure my father would only be working in Third and Second Districts, so there is that." He turned to his two ghostly friends, eyes softened with sadness. "Can we just stay like this for a little longer?"

The two ghosts tightened their grip and held on tight, giving all their strength, their love, and their compassion to their living friend.

Lenore and Naveh both growled at Hecate. "Why?" they asked as one, angry at their patron.

Hecate shivered, knowing fully well that, as powerful as she was, being one of the strongest deities there were in the new pantheon, they held enough combined power to fight a god of her caliber. Both were expert combatants and utterly ruthless in combat, the reason she chose them to become High Priests.

Centering herself, she gestured for them to sit down in her office, which they did. "It was unkind of me to force that meeting between Dante and his family, but it held a purpose. I would never force such a thing otherwise. Being a Mother is part of my core, and compassion and kindness and love and protectiveness toward children. But it was also that part of me that enforced that meeting. I am Mother to all children—to all people. I must stand for all. Sacrifice is part of my power, my purpose."

Naveh, who rarely cared much for others, crossed his arms and growled lightly. "Why then? No child should be forced into such a situation?"

"I needed to test the boy, to see if he was capable of deep, hard altruism. He is."

"For what purpose?" Lenore demanded.

"I need a mortal ambassador, someone untied to the immortal patterns and bloodlines. Humans are capable of greater change than we are, and they can see patterns that gods just cannot. I need that, and he is a perfect fit. It was that spark that first drew me to him. It is why I gave him the Silver Coin—my blessing made manifest."

"You want a child to be an ambassador?"

Hecate exploded, decades of worry and shame and pain and doubt and exhaustion all rising out of her. "I have no choice!" she commanded. "No one else fits, and I do not have time to find another, not with the war reaching a peak! That attack on the Third District is only the beginning, I foresee so much worse! Violence and pain torment! The Underworld is rising up as well. They may very well split from the pact, and if that happens, this world will become a wasteland! I need aid, now!"

Her words, loud and potent, held such power that her Chosen were cringing, their skins raised in goosebumps. If they had less power, both may have perished, their minds torn asunder by the force of her magic.

Lenore sighed. "It is still cruel. You owe the boy, as does Epione."

That deflated Hecate. "You are not wrong... Epione will help with his depression, blessing him and helping him make his potion work so he can actually access his magic. As for me, I will personally teach him to harness his Underworld powers. It is not much, but you know as well as I how little I can do. I swore to never give rampant blessings; they never go well when you are as powerful as I am. They can tear a soul apart. No... I will also grant to him an external blessing, a weapon or familiar or some sort of thing, something to help protect him in this war."

Lenore and Naveh shared a look before nodding. "We will do our part to help protect this child... How long does he have to become an ambassador?"

Hecate cringed. "I sent my Crone aspect to Hera. She demanded to see him in three months. So, we must prepare him and educate him on the current political structure, pathways, and problems. He must know the true depths of the war, what is really going on, why his village died, and by whom. He must know it all! We must also get him strong in magic, as strong as we can in three months. Most importantly, we must ask him to become the ambassador, and he must accept. If he does not... I am not sure that I alone can stop this war from escalating to apocalyptic proportions."

Dante followed Christopher and Alex out of his room and down the hall he lived in. "Where are we going?"

The ghosts shivered, with Alex saying, "We feel a pull. Someone with immeasurably powerful necromantic magics has summoned us. We cannot deny it."

Nodding, hesitant, Dante followed them back to the great libraries, to the circle he was tested at for affinities. Something had changed. In the circle was a black rectangle—a portal. From within, he saw Lenore's head pop out.

She smiled at him sadly, tipped her head, and said, "Come this way. Lady Hecate wants to speak with you."

Chest filled with quivering pain and fear, he followed into the portal after his ghostly friends. The world was filled with whispers and cool energy for the briefest of seconds before he appeared in a massive office, bigger than his room. The walls were covered in full bookcases. There was a roaring fireplace and magic symbols all over the walls. On one wall was a massive mirror swirling with smoke and shadows.

Finally, there was a desk, black and purple, and behind it was one stunning goddess. She looked different than before. Hecate seemed older, like forty or so, with skin the color of coal, hair covered in a wrap of dark rich blue. Her eyes were a soft reddish brown, and her lips were full. Teardrop tattoos made of blue ink led from her eyes. She was taller too, maybe six and a half feet tall. Her body was well muscled, more like a goddess of war. However, what caught Dante's attention most was the magical energy wafting off her in waves. Symbols of all of the old languages danced around her.

"Hello, dear sweet boy, it is an honor to see you once more." Her voice was deeper, rougher, but unbearably lovely. It warmed his skin and filled him with appreciation. "As it is an honor to meet your vassals, my sweet Christopher and the kind Alex."

Bowing, Dante spoke, "It is an honor to meet you as well, again, my lady."

Hecate laughed, then sighed. "I hope you will think so after I tell you why you are here." Before fear could fill him, she spoke, "You are not in trouble. I merely have an offer and an apology. Please listen with an open heart, my son, and make your choice."

Lenore, who had been quiet, approached and kneeled. "My love, you do not have to say yes. Answer her with mind and body and soul, not impulse."

And that only invoked greater fear. Gulping, Dante looked up. "Um... okay."

Hecate waved her hand, and a chair appeared. "Please, sit, and we will discuss everything." Dante did as she asked. "Let me be blunt. I am the reason you were forced to see your father once more, and here is why..."

And so Dante, wounded by her words, listened to her tale. His mind burned with every word, but still, he listened, and when she finished, he sat back.

"So, to recap..." he started. "The war is getting worse. The gods' egos are getting in the way, and you need me to help act as an ambassador to stem the tides... And you also needed to see if I could be altruistic and self-sacrificing, so you forced me to endure my father once more. Is that right?"

"More or less, sadly..."

Dante sighed, but really he already knew his answer. "When I offered myself to you, to become magical and a witch, I said I wanted to make the world a better place than when I left it. I haven't changed my mind... I accept your offer."

Hecate smiled radiantly. "I cannot express my pride, it is literally too much..." She stood tall. "Your studies may begin immediately. You no longer have to work in the Healing Wing as an aid. You will spend that time with me, learning the true history of our world—of the gods and how it has changed since Ragnarok. You will learn the hierarchy of the four realms. You will study the war and why it started.

"However, before that, I owe you a boon. No one should be forced to do what you did. I am Maiden, Mother, Crone. I know better. Ask of me and I will grant it. But be warned that I can only grant you one boon. Be careful to ask for the right thing. It could be anything... a familiar, a great weapon—"

Dante knew his request. "Can you revive Alex and Christopher?"

And the room went quiet... Everyone looking at Dante in shock...

Hecate spoke softly, "Yes, but can only help one of them. You must choose..."

"Christopher," Alex said, drawing their collective attention. He smiled, his eyes filled with aching pride. "He was a child when he passed. I lived some life; he barely had a moment, a blink of an eye..."

Dante turned to him. "Are you sure?"

"Yes, I am..." Alex turned to Hecate. "Do it. Revive Christopher."

"Dante, be warned once more. I can only grant you one boon. Is this truly what you want?" she asked.

Dante nodded. "Yes. A good friend is worth a thousand familiars, weapons, or spells. I never had much of a family, but I am gaining one by choice and chance. I choose that. "

Hecate clapped. "Then so be it." She strode to a stunned, silent Christopher and grabbed his face. "As Goddess of Necromancy, I grant to you the breath of life once more." She placed a kiss on his forehead, and dark energy exploded into the world, wrapping around his body and sinking in. As color faded back into the shadows, Christopher came back to life and Dante saw what he really looked like.

His eyes were wider and softer, his hair velvety and his skin tanned. He had more muscle than Dante had realized. He was shorter too, standing at half a foot shorter than he was. He was utterly adorable. It actually hurt to look at him; a weird tightening of his chest.

Tears filled Christopher's eyes. He stumbled, gasping for breath for a moment before exclaiming. "I'm alive! I'm alive!" He threw himself at Dante, hugging him tightly, kissing his cheek with great force. Pulling back, Dante saw that his eyes were a soft greenish brown and filled with tears. "Thank you so much... Thank you."

Dante smiled and shrugged. "I am just happy to help." He turned to Hecate. "He can come with me, right, when I am ambassador? Brighid told me about emotional support animals of the past. Why are there no emotional support humans?"

Hecate laughed. "Yes, he can, but he cannot have say in the meetings."

"What about Alex?"

"Of course... I am asking a lot of you. These are so small requests... Now, are you ready to get started?"

Dante nodded, standing as tall as he could. "As ready as I will ever be."

Ambassador to Be

Three months of hell began the moment Dante agreed to become the newest Ambassador. His days were packed with training, studying, and more training. Repeated exercises in moving small and large objects through difficult mazes, healing various wounds, learning how to sense and siphon pain, communing with the dead, astral-projecting intentionally, learning the basics of enchantment and divination (which was not as natural or easy as necromancy or healing by any means; the raw focus alone gave him horrible migraines), reading and sensing auras, creating dozens of spells for quick effect, mastering the bow, and so on.

He lost thirty pounds of fat, gained ten pounds of muscles, and two inches to his height. He slept like a rock every day, only to begin his suffering anew each night. When he wasn't training, he was studying the realities of the New Pantheon, and this is what he learned.

After Ragnarok, there was a second civil war as the gods from all realms tried to gain greater power still. Once the war passed, the gods realized they had to unite or go extinct. Hera married Baldur the Nordic God of Light and Love (and the only survivor of the Norse Pantheon, aside from Hela), and took over the survivors of the old splintered pantheons. When they took over, most gods retained their old positions. It was what they were good at, but only a handful of gods from most pantheons remained. Some were wiped out entirely, though he had not been told which ones. After returning to earth and seeing the horrors of how humans treated said earth, they decimated the population and took over.

Hera was still queen; she ordered the gods to repopulate and teach humans to respect nature and natural order. However, pollution of the Seas and all Freshwater was so bad that the Water gods begged for help; they were being poisoned by the taint. Denied and mocked, they rebelled and started the war, aiming to take over and heal their domain. The Underworld, over-crowded by humans' explosive population and a lack of Underworld gods, was close to doing the same, begging for aid as well but being denied it by the snooty, self-indulgent Sky gods.

It was to this that Dante was chosen to help, starting with the Underworld. Hecate could get them (the Underworld and Sky gods) to meet, but it was up to Dante, as an unbiased being, to make a final offering of help. He studied hard, learning of the various gods and spirits still around, all in a desperate attempt to fix the broken world and maybe end the war.

He had some ideas, two in particular, that would tie the Sky and Underworld, and maybe one that would help the Freshwater gods. It was a loose idea but one that he hoped would work. He shared it with no one, not even Hecate, not wanting to release his ideas until it was time. There was a reason for that, mainly the three main egos on the New Council—egos that would be particularly nightmarish, to begin with.

First, there was Hera, who was angry before but now was a nightmare of epic proportions. Rude, cold, and as power-hungry as before. She was also tremendously powerful, having absorbed a great deal of power from Zeus when he died… which apparently, many accused her of causing. She had grown comfortable in her power, but that was not what made her dangerous.

It was her mind; she was devious, smarter than Athena, and crueler than Ares. She had her own goals, goals no one knew.

Next was Aphrodite, whom Hecate said would hate him specifically for his asexuality. She had caused the death of Hippolytus in ancient times for the same reason, and he was just the famous example. She had butchered countless others for the so-called crime before or any other believed perversion of love. She was famous for her temper, abuse of power, and general cruelty. However, she was also the strongest person in the council period. As the daughter of Ouranos and being the literal incarnation of Love and Beauty, she wielded tremendous mystical power and was not afraid to use it.

Lastly was Athena, who took everything as an insult to her delicate ego. She was petty, cruel, hateful, and jealous of anyone with ideas that were not hers, or anyone that did well in a way she hadn't. Her punishment of Arachne was a great example; punishing the poor mortal for nothing more than pride, and defeating her in a weaving contest. She rarely listened to reason if her ego got in the way and would smite or curse anyone she felt slighted her. Most of the council hated her frankly; Hecate had to resist the urge to seal her mouth shut.

He worked hard to frame the ideas in such a way that no one could hate him for it, hurt him for it, or anything else. He could only hope he succeeded, having no interest in eternal torment or life as a tree, spider, or monster of whatever the gods wanted to turn him into.

"Are you ready?" Christopher asked, straightening Dante's tie for the third time. "You remembered your plans?"

Dante sighed, smiling at the fluttery sweetness of Christopher. Putting a hand on his cheek, he leaned in and rested his chin on the much shorter boy's head. "I am fine. Thank you for caring."

Christopher pouted. "Yeah, yeah, you are taller than I am, and so are most people. You're not special."

"You love me, and you know it."

Christopher said nothing, but he knew he was right. They were the best and closest of friends at that point. Christopher helped him to study, quizzing him on spells and magical ingredients and the divine hierarchy. They worked out together, practiced combat and archery, and in his rare moments of peace, they hung out with each other. He in turn helped Christopher adapt to life once more, and his growing magic. It was a great time and one that both of them dearly cherished.

"Dante, it's time." Both turned to face Hecate, who was standing at the doorway to Dante's room. "Are you ready?" she asked.

"As ready as I will ever be... Are you ready?"

Hecate smirked. "As much as I can imagine... Let's go."

She waved her hand and shadows wrapped around them, dispersing after a minute and revealing a large white marble door in a hall of white and gold marble, the walls and doors decorated with scenes of war and sex and violence so horrible and wonderful that Dante's eyes ached. They were more like memories etched into stone, but they were so clear that his mere mortal mind could not entirely handle them. He had to look away after just a moment, lest his mind be fried.

Christopher was gaping. "Your eyes are bloodshot!"

Hecate sighed. "I should have said something... I am used to only blessed beings entering these halls. The magic of the carvings invokes powerful memories, too powerful for mortal minds. I am so sorry."

"It's fine," Dante muttered.

Hecate shook her head. "It really isn't... Now, you must be careful. The gods are pure ego incarnate... Please, do not piss them off."

"I'll try..."

"Very well," Hecate sighed. "Christopher, remember you are allowed in but you can say nothing. You are only allowed through my blessing, nothing more. Do you understand?"

Christopher nodded. "Yes, Ma'am."

"Good. Now, let us enter."

And so they walked through the marble doors, which Dante realized were at least twenty feet tall. The moment they crossed the barrier, he shivered. His eyes widened as pure magic filled the air, magically charged with intent he could taste. Arrogance, hate, strength, love, doubt, fear, wisdom, and so on. It was missing one thing... one thing he was to bring. Something so important that Hecate sought a mere child out for it...

Humanity. Pure and beautiful humanity!

Well, that and the power to change. But still...

The Council Chamber was massive, a round arch with thrones of various makes in different segments. There were twelve seats, making up the New Council, and each person was extremely lovely.

First was Hera, and she was stunning. Built with a strong athletic frame, she was tanned and lovely with cascading black hair and the most flawless brown eyes that radiated warmth. Her face was so lovely that it was hard to describe past her eyes, and it kept shifting ever so slightly, which made sense given that she was pure energy made manifest, as were all gods. Her form was less stable. She was dressed in a lovely white dress that had a sash of gold to one side, the same colors as the marble.

Next to her was Baldur, dressed in similar colors. He was blue-eyed and so beautiful. Lean and lovely, with a tight shirt and pants, every single muscle was visible and perfect. He radiated warmth and light. His smile was genuine, and it lifted Dante's spirit.

On the distant left, he saw Aphrodite and she actually made his skin tingle, both with her power and beauty. She had straight brown hair, olive skin, and eyes that were a deep purple. She was built like an Amazon Warrior of Old, with strong muscle and a powerful straight stance. Hecate had told him that she was a war goddess in Sparta before she was fully worshipped by the whole Greek realm. So, it was natural that she looked like a warrior.

There were more people, of course, more gods and titans. The most interesting was the new placements—the gods and titans that had taken over for called gods. There was Helios, who had replaced Apollo on the Council, radiating a deep reviving light that made Dante smile. He was bold and beautiful with a strong jaw and aura of strength. There was Amaterasu who had replaced Dionysius and was currently dating the Moon goddess, Selene. She too radiated warmth comfort and kindness and healing energy with her stunning features and loving but very strong aura. There was Selene the Moon Goddess who had replaced Artemis. She was built like a warrior too, and her smile was more stoic than kind.

There was one empty seat, and that was for Poseidon, who had abdicated his seat during the Sea War.

All sky gods, other than Demeter and previously Poseidon before the war, are of some variety. No mix, blend, or representation. I need to change that.

Soon enough, Dante, Christopher, and Hecate were in the center of the Council Room. Drawing strength from the magic in the air through his breath, a trick Lenore taught him, Dante stood tall and let their power wash over him without burning him away.

Hecate made a sweeping bow. "Fellow Olympians, I bring to you my newest priest and ambassador, Dante. Though he is young, he is wise for his years and I foresee that he can offer enough to us to better our current collective path. Please lend him your ears and open your hearts to his words."

Dante too bowed, just in time for Hera to say, "So young... Well, I did agree to listen to his words. Please, stand and dazzle us, child. Prove your worth and wisdom." Her voice was soft and rich and imbued with tremendous power. It crashed against his very soul, threatening to obliterate his existence with just a tiny push.

He had to be good here, be perfect. His very reality was at stake. That and so many others... There was not a single inch of room for error.

It had to be perfect.

It had to be.

He had to be...

Humane
Suggestions

With radiant energy surging through his cells, Dante stood tall and spoke with the wisdom of human love.

"Divine Olympians, what I say, I say with piety and humanity. I speak from the heart, the soul, and mind."

He turned, and his eyes were immediately caught by the stunning visage of a goddess who he had missed before. He knew her to be Demeter, with her blonde hair and radiant air of instability. Her eyes bent with a fractured light, more than a few screws loose in her pretty head. He knew the stories; she had caused thousands of deaths after Persephone was captured by Hades, and yet she was a powerful ally of his, through Hecate. He had to impress her. She was naturally the strongest of the female goddesses born to Kronos and Rhea. There was a reason Zeus wanted her to be queen before he married Hera. Shaking off his momentary distraction, Dante turned back to the Council as a whole.

"My first suggestion, born through study and education is simple. It would be a gift, one to Hades that would serve to help his kingdom and link it forever to the Sky. The Gift I am speaking of... two goddesses to work in the Underworld, granting them a greater role and power, using their specific talents to heal the damage to the Underworld brought on by the previously booming human population."

The room went silent, but there was a clear tenseness in the air. Then Helios, blonde and beautiful, leaned forward. "What goddesses, kiddo?" He spoke with clarity and kindness, and real respect, so much so it startled Dante.

Hera gaped. "You cannot be serious, Helios! Give two goddesses to the trash heap that is Hades!"

Helios glared at her, and she backed down. Helios was more primordial than titan. He wasn't the God of the Sun, he was the sun, and that granted him great power and a greater form of immortality. He could not be stripped of his powers unlike a typical immortal. "The boy is loyal to his word, and as the Guardian of the Oaths, I respect that. Read his soul, as I have, you can see that his words are wise and his intentions as pure as fallen snow. Do not let your ego prevent the prevention of a devastating war you would likely never survive."

Hera gritted her teeth, as did Demeter, which made sense given Persephone's abduction and her past. "Fine. What goddesses did you have in mind, young Dante?"

With hesitation, Dante spoke, "Leto is first." Hera perked up then, looking almost smug. "She is the Titanness of Motherhood and Demurity. She is a light titan as well. She would be able to help care for and heal those children and parents stuck in the Fields of Asphodel, helping them to be reborn. Gods can be in more than one place at once, so really hiring her would be like hiring a dozen people at the least. Her healing essence, her light, would strengthen Persephone's life-giving essence as well, or well, in theory, she would."

Helios started to clap, pleased. "Very good, boy. Very good. I approve. Leto has been all but retired for eons. I think this would be good for her."

Athena, who had intentionally ignored, nodded. "I approve." Her tone was ice cold, so frigid it made the hearth and torches feel dimmer. "However, I do wonder who would be the other goddess you are proposing we send into the Underworld?"

Dante gathered his strength. "I... I propose you send Hebe into the Underworld."

Hera moved, then through her hand stretched out, she sent a white blast of magic at Dante. He knew it would have obliterated him to his soul, but before it reached him, a wall of shadow and a blast of sunlight stopped it.

Shaking, Dante turned and saw Hecate and Helios standing, glaring hatefully at Hera. "Hera, you dare attack my priest?" Hecate said, her tone ripping through the air with so much force that Dante's mind ached.

Every god and titan cringed, even Hera. "He dared propose my daughter, my youngest, enter the Underworld!" she yelled.

Hecate sneered. "The one you treated as a servant for centuries? It is pride that stops you, nothing more."

Helios nodded. "I agree. Now listen to his words. I sense he has a good idea brewing in that cute head of his."

Dante continued, "She is Goddess of Youth, Patron of Brides and Forgiveness. Why not make her the Goddess of Forgiveness as well? Help her guide those seeking forgiveness so they can be reborn, taking the strain off the Underworld. Collectively, Hebe and Leto would unwind the majority of issues in the Underworld, as those two places are the most severally in need of aid. Asphodel has the majority of people, followed by the Fields of Punishment. Together, not only would they do the most good, but they would also get tremendous power and influence, linking forever the Sky and the Underworld."

Helios clapped. "Well done, my boy. Well done. I approve."

Selene and Amaterasu did the same, nodding kindly toward Dante. Several other gods nodded, but Dante only looked briefly; he was too afraid to look away from Hera and be blasted again. He saw that, to his shock, Athena was nodding too. However, three heads were not...

Hera, Demeter, and Aphrodite. The latter of which sneered. "He is impure, a disgrace to love. I disapprove of all he says."

Hecate just sighed; she was annoyed but clearly unsurprised.

Demeter called out, "Send more vulnerable goddesses to Hades' domain? I do not think so!"

Hera scowled. "I would not send my daughter to the Underworld. Not now, not ever! But I am outvoted, and so to my great sadness, I will obey the will of the council." Power and order rippled through the council room as the order was declared. "Helios, since you agreed first, you can explain to those two why they are now doomed to the Underworld."

Helios sighed. "I figured you would do something like that. Very well."

Hera turned to Dante. "Go! Take our goddesses to the Underworld and explain to Hades why they come. They will swear in his service, should he accept..." Her head tipped to the side as if listening to something. "You have another idea, don't you? For Hades, I mean."

Dante sighed. "Yes, I will propose to him that some of his souls— those meant to be punished—be sent to clean out the rivers and lakes and streams. This would help the River gods and Naiads and so on, and in turn help Tethys and Oceanus, maybe opening them up to accepting my words as an ambassador. I hope that, by accepting me, I can help ease the war and make it so that so many do not have to suffer."

"You are a good soul, Dante," Helios said, his tone filled with genuine warmth beyond his literally sunny disposition. "I will send word ahead to Hades so he knows you are coming. Well done, my boy. Well done."

"Yes, well, this meeting is over," Hera declared, and the gods all vanished in a swirl of power, leaving Dante shaking and nearly collapsing.

Christopher was at his side, helping him to stand. "That was terrifying."

"Agreed..." Dante muttered.

Hecate nodded. "Yes, yes it was. Let's depart and ready ourselves for our next journey... To the Underworld, we go..."

The Second Fall

Descending into the Underworld, with Christopher's anchoring hand in his, Dante felt a sense of pride and peace. It was a simple thing, entering the House of Hades. It turned out Hecate had a literal doorway in her office that descended straight down. It was a peaceful route and one Dante enjoyed, mainly as he felt the welcoming cool touch of Underworld magic fill him.

He must have made some noise as Christopher turned to him. "Why are you sighing so happily?"

"Can't you feel it? The Underworld is all but saying hi!"

Christopher frowned. "I feel nothing but cold."

Hecate laughed. "Dante's ties to the Underworld are great, greater than most of my children, and I am the Goddess of Necromancy. It is natural that he feels welcomed in its embrace, just as you would feel around Gaia, dear Christopher. You possess an equally strong connection to the Earth, what with your potent animalistic magic."

Both boys nodded, with Dante feeling pleased. "I feel like my soul is being hugged, it's amazing!"

Hecate frowned this time. "That is odd... I have never heard of such a reaction. I will look into this." She turned her head further back to where two goddesses were walking. "How are you two holding up?"

They both sighed, then smiled with genuine warmth. Leto was the closest to them but strong and lean with perfect auburn hair that was laced into a tight braid. She had an aura of literal light about her, even in the dim air of the Underworld passage. Her eyes were a radiant gold, her skin tanned and olive. She was a rare beauty, even by god standards, which made sense seeing as she had produced two of the most powerful deities by Zeus.

Then there was Hebe, her mother's clone with her dark hair and wide brown eyes, only slimmer and more awkward, like a perpetual teenager. She was beyond lovely and radiated vast power that shimmed and simmered in the air around her. Her parents, being two potent gods, had clearly granted her great strength. However, she held an air of inexperience and nervousness; she had never been granted powerful positions by her parents, and she had been treated as a servant for so long and it showed.

They would make wonderful additions to the Underworld, Dante knew he had made the right choice...

Hebe spoke first, her voice cracking slightly. "I am nervous, but I appreciate the chance to make something more of myself. For far too long, I have been pushed aside." She smiled at Dante, brushing his face with her hand. "You spoke wisely. Helios showed me what you said. I appreciate that you actually considered me when, for far too long, I have been ignored, especially by my own blood."

Leto nodded. "After having my twins..." They all cringed. The memory of how the twins perished in the civil war was a haunting one, especially for their mother. "I was all but ignored by everyone. I had no real position. I was barely acknowledged, even by mortals, and I was constantly abused by

Hera. No... I never thought to work for Hades, but I never hated him like the majority of gods. I foresee only positive things coming from this path. She is right, you are wise, my son."

Flushed, Dante turned away, feeling Christopher squeezing his hand in pride.

"She's right. They both are. You did really, really well," Christopher remarked.

Dante squeezed right back, unable to trust his words.

They said nothing more for the rest of the trip, which took about half an hour. Soon they were in a bank of foggy magic, pure Underworld magic that Dante happily breathed in. His skin tingled with dark magic, his soul quivering from the raw acceptance he felt within. The fog did fade soon, and they all finally saw the palace of Hades.

It was massive; made of black stones like Hecate's temple, with marbled cracks of silver, gold, and bronze. Random gems peppered the wall, as well as sacred runes. Scenes covered the walls as well, but much as with the scenes of New Olympus, he could not see them with his mortal eyes as they invoked memories so old and strong that they could wipe his mind away. He had to look away and focus as they hurried toward the gates and doors within.

As they entered the gates, Dante saw the garden of Persephone, which naturally included the legendary pomegranates. There were flowers and bushes and trees of all sorts; some he recognized, many he did not, all of which only sustained themselves through the inherited light and life of Persephone and the power she held within.

"Oh, they are beautiful!" Hebe said as she and Leto approached the garden. In an instant, their extra powerful auras radiated outward, and every single flower, bush, and tree perked right up, their presence drinking in the power of the two Sky gods. The perfume of the garden magnified to dizzying proportions, the presence of light and beauty magnified to inhumane levels, as did the presence of life.

Delighted feminine laughter drew them to the far gate, where three beings were standing. Each powerful god and terrifying figure, and yet Dante did not feel afraid.

The first was a man, extremely tall with a strong brow and jaw. He had silky black hair and a lovely beard. He oozed dark power and a sense of strength that Dante doubted he could ever hope to match. He had in his hands a bident and a clear willingness to use it. The man was glaring at them all, with suspicion more than aggression.

The next was a woman, half corpse, half stunning woman. She radiated cold and power and ruthlessness. This was Hela, the Norse Goddess of Death and one of the only survivors of her Pantheon. She, according to Hecate, became part of the Head Trio of the Underworld, ruling Asphodel specifically with a cold icy grip. She hadn't been mentioned in the books he read on the Underworld, as those books were written before that happened. They had merely been translated into the universal language.

Last and most striking of all was Persephone. Blonde and beautiful, she had the most stunning bluish grey eyes. Dressed in yellow pastel, she had the kindest of smiles. She was tall, taller than her husband even, and she oozed a mixture of Dark Underworld power, Potent Sky magic, Mild Ocean Potency, and Divesting Earth energy. Her aura was greater by far than even both Hades and Hela combined.

Dante gaped at her. "You feel like me!"

Persephone giggled. "Technically I am older, so you feel like me... But yes, your aura is a great deal like my own. Like me, you hold sway over all four realms, with Earth and Underworld being your greatest of powers." She hurried forth and pulled him into a loving embrace. "It is so nice to meet one like me. Oh, and you are so cute—both of you!" She repeated the same act with Christopher, then Hecate and Hebe. "Hecate, it has been far too long, and you too, Hebe. Leto, you are always welcome in my home... But I must ask, why are you all here?"

Dante shivered as all eyes moved to him. "My lady... I am the ambassador to Hecate, and I come with a proposal... if you and your beloveds are willing to hear it."

"Naturally, please... Why not enjoy a meal while we speak?" She snapped her fingers, and a picnic table appeared, covered in food. "Do not worry about being bound to my realm. I imported the meal from my mother's kitchen." And so they ate and drank and laughed, soothing the majority of Dante's worries, at least until Persephone said, " So, Dante, what is it that you wish to tell us? How did you become a Priest and Ambassador and Witch? I sense no divine blood or blessing in you."

And so Dante wove his tale, every detail, hoping to win over the gods of the Underworld...

Hecate worried for a moment, as she watched her beloved friend Persephone listen to Dante. Few knew it, but the queen ruled the Underworld, not Hades. It had been that way for eons. She was wiser, stronger and at times far, far meaner. She held the strength of her divine parents, and unlike most, she drew power from all realms, that included the wisdom of Gaia herself. She was not one to trifle with, even Hera would hesitate with all her new power. However, as she watched and listened, she felt hope as her beloved friend smiled at the boy with warmth and acceptance.

Persephone reached over, grabbing Dante's hand. "You are a strong soul... I think Hebe and Leto will make tremendous additions to our realm, and I approve of the usage of souls stuck in punishment to serve in cleaning bodies of freshwater. It would help the Underworld by stemming the flow of dead souls into our realm... and it might help end the war, or at least get the Water gods to listen and reason."

Hades nodded. "I concur, wife. It would be wise."

Hela smiled. "I cannot argue, this can only be good... Leto, you will technically be serving me, as I hold sway over the Fields of Asphodel. The oaths are quite simple and will imbue you with a connection to the Underworld and its majesty. Breaking those oaths would be quite dangerous. Be clear on that."

Leto nodded, bowing her head softly. "I would be honored to make those oaths."

"As would I," Hebe echoed.

"Wonderful!" Persephone clapped her hands, delighted. "Now, since you came all this way, you might as well sleep the night here. I will have beds arranged for you. I would like to speak to Dante in private, if that is all right, Hecate."

That terrified the Goddess of Magic, but she knew better than to deny her old friend. She put on a false smile. "Never an issue, Persephone."

The queen stood and held out her hand for Dante to grab. "Come with me, little love."

Dante grabbed her hand, only to be swept away in a swirl of shadow and the scent of vanilla.

Christopher paled. *Please tell me he will be okay,* he prayed.

Hecate sighed. "I hope so," she whispered.

Fertile Advice

As he moved through the shadows, the air and magic and radiant energy filled the world with the scent of vanilla and oranges and cinnamon; a heady, warm, comfortable scent that was so enticing that he ended up leaning into it and thus into a very amused Persephone. He tried to recoil in shock and terror, but she held him fast.

"It is fine. My aura has that effect on others. You should see how it affects people with less control than you." Her eyes shifted, turning less gold and more amber. Her features solidified into something less shimmery as her aura toned down, becoming more human. As this happened, her scent diminished to manageable levels. "There, that should be better."

Dante nodded, masking his fear as much as he could. "Thank you, my lady." He looked around and realized they were in a hall, void of others.

"Please, just Persephone. You are Hecate's child, born of her admiration, and she is all but a sister to me—a mother as well, more than Demeter ever was." She sneered.

"Huh? I thought you loved your mother?"

Persephone's brow quirked. "That is what the stories say, but no. Remember how I was conceived? I was the child of assault; Zeus brutalized my mother as a snake. She hated me for some time, just as she hated Arion and Despoina who were born to the assault of Poseidon. No, she only cared for me in truth once Hades took me. And do you know why Hades took me...? I can give you a hint: he is as asexual as I sense you are."

Dante shivered. "He is a just god—one of the few—and he is a judge of the dead. You are stunning. Rarely so. Some god wanted you in a way you, as a child, were not ready for?"

Persephone's eyes widened. "You are bright, yes that is what happened. It was not just any god though, it was my own father. Zeus wanted me, and so Hades pulled strings to save me. He took me as his bride but never touched me. Why do you think I fell in love, even after he took me? My mother had all but imprisoned me. I lived in a gilded cage and I hated it. He set me free, never harming or hating or mistreating me. He spoke to me as an equal; all Underworld gods did. They are not perfect. Hypnos is a trickster. He is quite lazy and kind of sexist. All children of Nyx are spoiled. Hades has a terrible temper, as do I if I am being honest. However, it was their decency that won my heart. I loved them and they loved me.

I married Hades after some time down here, in part to protect myself, and also to connect with someone that treated me as an equal for the first time, and to live where I was not mocked for being a mere Flower Goddess, or leered at for being beautiful, or called nasty things for being unavailable or spoiled. I was treated like a goddess, a queen, worthy and proud. When I bound myself to Hades and the Underworld, my powers rippled through the world and allowed a garden to grow. I was, for a time, happy.

My mother ruined it by slaughtering thousands in a hissy fit! I hate harming others; it is not in my nature. I was forced back by Zeus, but I knew the rules of the Underworld, and even if I did not, I am the Goddess of Flowers raised by the Goddess of Agriculture and the Earth. I knew, just looking at the fruit, born of a flowering plant, that I would be bound to the Underworld. I ate it willingly. I ensured my return! I took command of my destiny. I molded my path. No one, not even my mother or father or husband, would take that from me! I did it!"

Dante nodded slowly. "Why was the story so warped?"

Persephone sighed, sitting down on the ground. "There used to be things called telephones in the time before we took over. They allowed for mass communication, like Hecate's mirror or other such enchantments. There was a game, the telephone game, where you whispered into one person's ear a sentence. They repeated to another and another and so on until the last person shouted out the words. It was always wrong. When a story passes on, especially warped and spoken of by people that have a negative tie to it, things change. The damage is done. People and gods believe only what they choose to believe. I cannot change this entirely but I wanted you to know."

"Why?"

She gave a pained smile. "I want you to see that you can mold your own path. You can be more than what we cold, cruel, vile gods can be." She looked up at him with tears. "I am the Queen of the Underworld. I listen to every soul that is judged, or at least I try to. I take petitions and hear horrible stories. I know of the gods' evil more than most." She wiped aside the tears that came to her eyes. " However, the other reason I tell you this is to remember that no story, no myth, is accurate. So much happened, both due to the telephone game but also due to the power of gossip and hate and the power that comes from being the victor and the one controlling the narrative. That will serve you well as an ambassador. Question everything, always!"

Touched, Dante kneeled to her. "Thank you, Persephone."

"Never a problem. Oh, and feel free to share this story with your little friend, but do not be surprised if he doubts the tale... Now we ought to be getting back; they might think I have eaten you or turned you into a poplar or mint."

They shared a chuckle and teleported back, where they saw the collective looking at them with worry and confusion.

Persephone smiled. "Don't worry, Hecate. He is fine. We just shared a conversation. Now, you should all be heading for bed, the Underworld's raw power can be straining to mortal souls... Hebe, Leto, come with me and make your oaths. Hades will lead you to your rooms, boys."

They all stood and started away with the brooding god leading them to their rooms. Dante, as they traveled, considered the tale of Persephone and wondered just how it would end up helping in the future. Could he use it? He sort of felt like he had to...

The Warmth
of Hades

Hades, now that he was less broody and cold, was a stunning man of perfect masculine beauty. Dante got a closer look and could not help but flush a little. His brow was strong, as was his square jaw, covered in a thick curly matt of hair. His hair was almost purple; it was so black, and it held a lovely shine to it. He had a lovely smile behind his beard, warm and kind with his thin lips. His nose was straight and hawkish. He oozed masculine energy; it poured from every pore in an undeniably beautiful way.

However, the real attention grabber was his smile. There were laugh lines on his face, and crow's feet; he almost seemed human. It was almost distracting, but it changed his beauty from alluring to comforting. He looked like a parental figure, not a walking fantasy. He still held a warrior's build, but there was a softness to him that made him pleasing to be around.

"See something interesting, child?" Hades suddenly asked in a rather amused way, making Dante jump. The god then laughed. "You are not very subtle. You know that, right?"

Dante sighed. "Apparently, not."

"I am aware of my beauty, child. You should not be ashamed for noticing," Hades said, warm and sweet as could be.

"It was more your paternal air, not your beauty that caught my eyes."

The man stopped, turning to him with warmth. "Not many notice that. They focus on my godly good looks. I am the child of Rhea; she would not and could not produce ugly children. If you saw her, you'd understand. You might see her today; she comes and goes as she wants. My mother is a flighty soul." There was an edge to his voice, of something akin to hate, that Dante noticed. "Never mind that. Tell me, my boy, have you tried practicing your Underworld magic here?"

Date shook his head. " Not yet, I haven't had the chance."

Christopher, silent with fear, piped up, "I have been too nervous. I cannot feel the earth here, my powers feel stemmed."

Hades chuckled for a moment. "You are thinking of your powers backward, I suspect. You cannot reach down for your power but up. Imagine you are a tree, drinking in the powers of Gaia like you would the Helios' rays."

Dante nodded and did just that, feeling Christopher doing the same, and both started to glow softly a radiant green color. The power was muted, the Underworld's essence was far too great to feel much through it, but he could in fact feel Gaia's majesty.

Christopher beamed at Hades. "Thank you, my lord."

"You are most welcome," Hades said, his tone like a full embrace. He turned to Dante. "I would be most careful when drawing on my domain just yet. Wait until you have the protection of myself or my wife or Hela or Hecate. The power of my domain is greater here—in my seat of power—and it could pull you fully from your body before you are ready, forcing you to tap into powers you have yet to manifest." He frowned. "What powers have you manifested?"

"Underworld magic?" Dante asked, getting a nod. "Well... communing with the dead, for one, though only in theory... Astral-projecting intentionally, though again mostly in theory, as I am still human. Reading and sensing auras is the thing I am best at so far, but I have to really focus. It has only been about three months that I have trained in Underworld magic so deeply."

The man nodded. "I see... For three months, that is good. I would not use the aura sensing here, at all, it might kill you. You may be able to see my full form, or that of any immortal here, which could and would be fatal. You know the tale of Semele, I am sure." Both boys nodded. "Communing with the dead could also be difficult. The dead are stronger than the living. You may unintentionally give too much of yourself when you try. You must be very very cautious."

Dante sighed. "I wish someone would have warned me."

"You are pure human, and you bear a rare affinity for the Underworld. It is such an uncommon combination that I think people, Hecate included, forget to do their diligence. Well, at the least you know now." He smiled. "Let us hurry to your room, my boys."

"Our room?" Dante and Christopher asked as one.

Hades smirked, a lovely expression of pure mischief. "Didn't I say that you would be sharing a room?"

And like that, Hades led the stunned duo to their room, which was beautiful. The walls were the same marbled black as before, with no images to burn out Dante's brain. Two large purple-clothed beds lay side by side. A roaring fireplace burned merrily on the opposite side of the room. Most interestingly, there were runes floating in the air, symbols of power and protection and peace that he felt radiating and filtering the magic of the Underworld.

"What do these do?" Dante asked, pointing at the runes. "I can feel their protective magic. Their aura is innately strong but I do not know enough of enchantment to know their purpose."

Hades' smile was radiant. "They protect your thoughts and minds from the side effects of the Underworld's magic. You are at no risk of astral-projecting or forced future-seeing or empathy here. You are sheltered from your subconscious reacting to our magic, or worse, forces summoning your spirit against your will."

Dante beamed. "Thank you for that. I really appreciate that."

"It is no trouble. Sleep well, boys, and know you have our blessing."

The doors closed behind him and Dante stretched. "Time for a bath, then bed. I am beat... Two divine meetings in one day. I can still feel their magic in my skin."

Christopher laughed, then sighed deeply. "Same... How are you not terrified right now? We are in the Underworld!"

Dante shrugged. "Not sure really... Just not. I guess I don't see death as evil or bad; it is the same with the gods here."

"I guess... "

Divine Promises, Friendly Vows

In the Underworld Throne room, the goddesses congregated and waited for Hades to return. No matter how frequently Persephone had been in the room, she always felt profoundly moved by its beauty and strength. Sacred Amber, a gift from Gaia herself, peppered the walls alongside bones and amethysts and turquoise and silver. The magic resonated alongside scenes of Hades taking over the Underworld, the Mortal Deads' first descent into the House of Hades, Persephone's descent into the Underworld, Hecate's gracious time as her attendant, and so many other scenes. The memories were strong, even for a powerful deity as she was.

Persephone sat on one of the three thrones, her in the center, made of shadows and silver in the shape of flowers of various types. It radiated her strength, for it was the literal seat of her power. Before her, stood the goddesses Leto, Hebe, and Hecate. To her left was Hela, sitting on a throne forged from ice and mist, with skulls echoing throughout it. To her right was Hades' throne, and it was tall and bronze, etched with symbols of power and peace. Combined, they were so powerful that they rendered the air warped with strength and might and dark energy. Even Hebe, who was actually rather powerful, shivered at its majesty.

"I sense the boys have been placed to bed. My lord will be here shortly," Persephone said, standing straighter as she looked at Hecate. "You placed a vast burden on a mere mortal, but I know you well enough to know your purpose was pure. I pray he forgives you someday. Really? Forcing him to care for his abusive family..." She sighed. "But, enough of that. He is interesting, but this is more important. It is time for you two"—she nodded to Hebe and Leto—"to fulfill your sacred vows."

The two goddesses, radiant and tall, fell to a knee before Persephone. Their magic opened up, flooding the world with tremendous power just as Hades appeared in the room. Without saying a word, he hurried to his throne and sat down elegantly. With all Head gods present, the vows could be said.

And so they were, in ancient tongues no mortal could speak, a language so old Gaia herself first spoke it to Nyx and Ouranos and later her children. Each syllable was so powerful that the room shook from the force. Any mere humans present would have evaporated from the pressure, even if they had divine blood or blessing. The vows took nearly an hour to recite, covering all bases and clarifying connection, power, and loyalty so potently that it rewrote the goddesses' makeup.

Leto was first affected, her older power more sensitive to the changes. Her eyes, a shimmering gold, turned darker to an amber tone. Though she did not lose her light, her dark connection magnified a hundredfold. Her very shadow seemed to deepen. Overall, she went from a mildly powerful goddess, just above average, to one comparable to the late Dionysius.

Hebe, already great due to her divine heritage, exploded into power like an earthquake. She let out a long moan, her skin vibrating with the weight of her new connection. She held her head, and Persephone knew that she was now hearing the prayers of those spirits begging for forgiveness. Her mind would and was expanding to compensate for the strain.

The two goddesses fainted, the power overwhelming them. They woke in moments, mere moments, standing with limbs overflowing with energy.

"That was incredible!" Leto said. "I feel so much power in my body..." Her eyes widened. "My light, I feel it infusing into the Underworld!"

"Same with mine!" Hebe uttered, her tone awed.

Hecate, ever the teacher, nodded. "When you bind to any plain, you share what you have. You were not born to your domains, so you did not notice, but connecting to a secondary realm, you are able to feel the blending of power as you link to the Underworld. Persephone's Garden is now going to be ten times as lovely, what with the essence of Youth and Life and Light infusing itself into the very air and soil."

Hebe beamed. "I am honored. It was such a lovely garden..."

"As am I... When do we get started?" Leto asked. "I have not been allowed to act on my domain in eons; Hera never allowed it." Her tone shifted, turning hateful.

"We all know Hera is awful... you may begin tomorrow. You need to adapt to your powers; a nice night's sleep will do you well. Go have good dreams. Let your power sink into your essence, your body and mind becoming full once more." She clapped her hands, summoning two spirits. "Lead these ladies to their new rooms."

Nodding, the two new Underworld goddesses bowed to their new queen and followed the spirits out of the throne room, their steps weary and woozy as they struggled to handle the explosive magic in their essence.

"So, you don't have a talisman?" Dante asked, looking at his shirtless friend as he cuddled into his bed. He realized, for the first time, that Christopher had no jewelry on his body. No trace of a talisman to be found.

Christopher blinked at him, smiling. "I forgot how you know about divine blood. Being Hecate's legacy, my blood is basically a talisman, less so than my mother's, but still, it helps me focus my magic."

Excitement filled Dante. "I'll make you one for protection if nothing else! I mean, your blood focuses your magic but it does not give you mystical protection."

Christopher flushed, his tanned skin turning a dark red. Then, without prompting, he hopped off his bed and hustled over to Dante. He pulled him off his bed, which made Dante a bit confused. Before Dante could ask what he wanted, he buried himself into Dante's thankfully clothed chest. "Why are you so good to me...?"

Dante would have said something, anything, but before he could, Christopher leaned up and kissed him. It was soft and kind and transmitted nothing but warmth and trust and a sense of love that left Dante breathless.

Leaning down, Dante pressed back, kissing Christopher right back. It was awkward and messy, but so were they—just shy of fifteen and entirely new to the world of romance. Still, it was beautiful.

As they pulled back, panting a bit, both boys flushed at each other and smiled.

Dante cleared his throat. "So... do you usually attack your friends with kisses?" He teased.

"Not my friends, no."

And they laughed and laughed and laughed.

Then Dante said, "Christopher, even if this part of our lives does not work out... do not stop being my friend. So many people do that."

Christopher held out his hand and they shook. "Deal."

And the pact was born, one of new, innocent love...

Dante could only hope it lasted. Be it friendly or more, he could only hope it lasted.

Before they went to bed, separately, they may have kissed a bit more, holding fast to the promise and the comfort that it brought.

A Different Mother's Request

The room Dante was sleeping in was set to be protected from any form of astral projection and such. So, naturally, he was torn from his body the moment he fell asleep, with no dreams to act as an intermediary. It wasn't painful though, it was pleasant and warm, a mother's loving embrace simply tugging him from his flesh. Turning as he rose, he saw himself smiling without bleeding eyes, a slight glow of gold and green around his skin.

Turning back around, he flew at speeds that should have left him nauseous but did not. He blasted away out of the House of Hades at such speeds that he could see nothing specific except a blur of color and magic, and just as fast he rushed toward the cavernous ceiling of the Underworld proper, which finally made him scream in shock.

The moment he thrust through the underbelly of the earth, everything changed. Peace and love overwhelmed his soul, so strong that it made him cry. He shook and searched for the source in the darkness, only to at first see nothing. The world around him shimmered and sifted, and then a woman's face appeared in front of him. She was heavy set and extremely curvy, and every pound of her was lovely. Her skin was the color of healthy red dirt, her eyes the same brown as Hera's, only filled with a thousand times more love and hate all at once. She had a smile with wide thin lips and a hawkish nose. Her hair was made of roots and vines, almost like dredlocks, only a mixture of white and red and black. She was also naked, very, very naked.

So, being the respectful young man he was, he focused solely on her smile, which was not hard, as she had a lovely, flawless smile that made Aphrodite look flat-out homely.

"Hello, my sweet, loving, loyal son." Her voice hummed around him, filled to the brim with enough power to devour the entire Olympian and Underworld council at once. Even as a mere astral body, he could taste her rage, her familiar majesty and—

"GAIA!" Dante coughed out, wide-eyed and terrified. He went to bow but she stopped him with her arms, pulling him in close enough to kiss his forehead. Immediately her power surged through him, soaking up his fear and doubt.

"My son, you never have to bow, none of my precious humans have to. When foolish Zeus butchered your people in a flood, it was I who restored you with my very bones. It was I who chose to allow you to remain connected through magic to my Earth. It is I who continue to empower you, my sweet, as a healer. I have watched you your whole life, as I watch all my mortal children, and now I ask of you a boon."

Dante stopped, looking at her seriously. "Can I guess?"

She nodded. "Please do."

"The Earth is as damaged as the Seas, but no one offers to help. Only the Sky, or rather the Heavens, are free from the damage."

Gaia smiled, a mother's pride echoing in her features. "You are mostly right. The skies are damaged, but as the Heavens are the seat of the portal to the home of the gods, more radiant energy flows through it. It is why you draw radiant energy through the air. Combined with the gods' presence, it has healed the sky almost entirely. However, we are not so lucky, Earth and Seas... and this is why I beseech your aid."

Dante nodded, eyes as serious as could be. "How do I help?"

"The Earth children are scattered and wild. They lack structure. They need guidance and order. As an ambassador and a child of my magic, you hold sway over them alongside your Christopher. You must guide them as well. Move them to order, lest the damage destroys their source connection to me. Satyrs, Centaurs, Maenads, Nymphs, and so on... Even Demeter and Persephone are at risk; they draw so heavily on my essence for power. You must help me, and soon."

"Okay... I will do what I have to, but don't I need Olympian permission?"

She laughed, her tone cold as a glacier. "I am the Earth itself. My will supersedes them, but you are not entirely wrong. I will send a message to a Nymph living in New Olympus. She will speak to them for me. Do not worry about her being harmed, my blessing will be upon her, easily thwarting even Hera's petty, paltry magic."

"That is a relief." To be honest, that was in fact a worry of his. The gods were not known for their kindness, or willingness to obey anyone but their own egos. "So... what now?"

Gaia turned to him, turning her arm over. A purple rock appeared in her hand. "This is a chunk of Amethyst straight from my womb. I think Christopher might indeed want this as part of his talisman. Consider it a down payment for aiding me in this task." She placed it in his hand. "Now, this is important. As my son and one with a strong connection to magic, even if you cannot tap into your body's power yet, and solely rely on the power of the world around you, you can follow the marks of pain emanating from my body and soul. You can sense pollution and its costs. You can sense my children who are sick, weary, and unstable. Find those that can help, and use that deep wisdom that infills you so deeply to help me. It is all I can do to not collapse under the damage of human deeds from the times before the gods returned." She sighed, shaking their small room. "You must return. It is time for you to sleep and rest. And when you wake, you can express the fullness of your mission." She frowned. "Do you swear to me that you will help?"

"Yes, I do, Mother."

"Good... good... I will not ask an oath on Styx. I trust your word, as Helios said you hold fast to what you say. Know that you carry my love and my blessing, dear boy."

She waved her hand and the world blurred and darkness overwhelmed him once more, this time the darkness of Morpheus' magic as he entered the realm of sleep. As he slept, the weight of his new mission, the mark of duty on his soul, weighed heavily.

Why me... why me?

"You are handling this really well," Hades said as he watched Dante bless the talisman he was forging for Christopher with Amethyst he had been given from Gaia herself. "Most would be losing their minds, begging!"

Dante sighed, and when he turned, Hades stepped back. His powers as the Great Judge were not needed to see the soul-deep weariness in the boy's eyes. The part of Hades that was a father, that had raised three goddesses and watched over countless children, broke for the boy.

"I am tired. I am already depressed, but I have no choice. My sanity, my safety, my existence is not as important as the greater whole." The boy shrugged, with exhaustion and misery so present in his every cell. "I want to cry, to freak out, to whine and express my rag. But honestly, what is the point? Even if I did, would the gods care? And if they did, it would be forced onto someone else. This is my duty now. I choose to bear it and I want to help. Besides, I asked for this. I asked Hecate to give me the chance to make the world better..."

With one hand, Hades gripped Dante's shoulder. "You are a good kid. We do not deserve you. None of us." Dante smiled at him, though weary and sore, it was genuine and lifted Hades' spirit ever so slightly. Then, he turned back to the talisman and pushed his magic into it. Silvery grey magic filled the air. "How did you learn this? It is more advanced than you ought to be for your current abilities?"

Dante giggled. "My mentor, Naveh, taught me in case my talisman was destroyed. He went through three of them before Nanuk was made. It is hard to cast, but my focus is really strong and I have a potent will. My head will ache for like two or three hours but it will be worth it."

The father in Hades' heart surged forth. "So you like the boy?"

Dante flushed. "Yeah, I do... He's sweet and funny and... he is nice. I like looking at him too, which is always good. And though he is quiet at times, he is really smart. I just wish he would act on it more. Most people are not as smart as I am. I am not bragging, it's just true, but he is easily my equal and I love it."

"I wish you well then, my son." The light of Dante's magic faded, and Hades saw the beautiful talisman before him. It was silver and purple and etched with spirals of blood. It radiated potent Earth magic, the essence of Gaia's majesty. "Well done!"

Dante swayed for a moment, then stood up with a radiant smile. "See, I did it. I just wish Radiant energy was easier to draw on here vs pure Underworld magic. Let's get this to Christopher!" The boy grabbed the talisman and marched off, happy as could be.

Hades sighed. "I really hope the boy manages to survive us and makes the difference he seeks in the world."

"It's lovely!" Christopher said, happily placing the talisman over his neck. He felt the simmering energy rushing over his skin, powerful mystic strength that lingered over his body. He could sense the protective energy, the impressive will imbued into the magics. "I could never make something like this. I am so jealous of your affinities! I mean I love my affinity for animals, but still, I would love to be able to do more!"

Dante laughed. "You can do whatever you put your mind to, Christopher. Technically my affinity is just the result of having a strong will. I am not magically gifted in anything, I'm just less likely to screw up on those areas."

"Fair enough. Maybe you can tutor me." Christopher leaned in, pecking Dante's oddly soft lips once. "I think you'd make a great teacher."

Dante blushed. "Maybe I would." His tone was soft, not quite scared but definitely shy. It was utterly loveable and adorable.

Christopher laughed. He adored how easily the powerful boy before him blushed or shied away from compliments. Dante had no clue of how good he was, how rare it was to find even a blessed child of Hecate with the raw skill he seemed to have for magic. Sure, affinities were not inherited gifts in magic, they are just suggestions of where you might do well, but when Dante tried he excelled. His healing skills and potent ties to the Underworld were tremendous. He would likely not need to draw on Radiant energy in a year or so, an almost unheard of speed. When that happened, he would be scarily dangerous... like demigod dangerous...

This only made Christopher want to train more, fight more, and be better. And so, with that in mind, he stood as tall as his tiny frame allowed. With his talisman on his chest, he uttered the words that would change his path.

"I want to help you, Dante. As ambassador, I mean. I can command animals. I can heal a little since I trained with you. I am not a weak warrior. I want to act as your guardian, your warrior. Not just cos I want to date you, I see how powerful your mission is and I know you cannot do it on your own. You are at risk, you need protection, and I want to be a part of that. Now and forever, no matter what happens to our new love."

The air rippled as Christopher infused his words with his passion and power. Dante, with wide eyes, clearly sensed the power of his oath. "You really mean that... don't you?"

He nodded and fell to one knee. "Please, accept my oath. Make it binding. You gave me life, now give me purpose."

"Why me?" Dante begged.

"You are kind, you are strong, you sacrifice yourself for the world at large. You gave me life, you gave me a friend and maybe something more."

There was a moment of silence, and then Dante nodded, tears in his eyes. "I accept your oath as binding, for as long as both of us desire it."

And the magic invoked linked the two, just as purely as the power of the Styx, marking their very souls. Dante helped him to stand, and as they embraced, they heard the soft clapping of Hecate behind them.

"Very, very well done, Christopher..."

Christopher flushed at his grandma's words. "Do you think I made the right choice?"

"You saw a need and you set forth to fulfill it. Dante cannot always be guarded by the gods. Yes, for some time, but one day he must seek out change on his own. He is not a warrior, he will need a protector, a guard... and for that purpose, I grant you this." Hecate clapped her hands together, causing light to form, and from within that light, something formed...

A familiar shape...

A dog!

"It's a puppy!" Dante said, excited.

"It is," she said. "One of my puppies. And so, it is mystical. But it is not Christopher or your pet Dante, it is your joined familiar, born of that oath and your new connection. It will respond to your commands—both of yours—and will grow to be a fervent protector and guide. Never abuse it, for it is part of you."

The light fully faded as Christopher saw what it looked like. It was orange, oddly, with a white patch on his throat and belly. It looked like an orange cat, but it was a dog. He laughed a little, happily taking the puppy from his grandma. The moment his skin touched the beast, he felt a heavy magic binding them, something he was sure Dante felt when he reached forward to pet him.

"What should we call him?" Dante asked.

"When I was little, I used to imagine having my own familiar named Ghost... But I think you should have a say in his name."

Dante beamed. "He is a little gentleman, what with his little bowtie..." He gestured to the white patch on his throat. "So from now on, he is Mr. Ghost!"

They shared laughter as the magic of a name settled into the beast, binding the three of them even closer together.

And so they stood; warrior, ambassador, familiar and goddess, happy and peaceful and ready for the struggles to come.

Hecate put on a proud face to hide her worry as she watched. Dante curled around the adorable, now squealing puppy. They cooed and loved it dearly, telling it how much they cared and adored its perfect face. She wondered, absently, why it was cat-colored, but that mattered far less than Christopher's choice.

Christopher made the right choice, making purpose in his second life. I am so proud. But was it right? The world, the balance, is so at risk...

Sighing, she focused on their oath, the new magic formed of trust and new love, and it made her smile.

If there are powers greater than the gods, please let it last, please let it keep them both safe...

An Unholy Reminder

"It's lovely," Christopher said, looking warmly at the River Lethe before him.

Hades and Persephone had decided to give them a view of the most sacred of rivers since it was their last few moments in the Underworld. Lethe and Styx— the River of Forgetfulness and the River of Hate—were natural opposites. Lethe was pure white, rushing by at the pace of a snail, sluggish and slow and bored, drinking up light and magic as it passed by. Styx was a rapid river, screaming by and gushing black foam on everything with a strong emotional heat oozing off its waters.

Dante, standing a bit behind Christopher, nodded. "It is... Two marvels so few had ever or will ever see."

"Thank you."

The boys both jumped in shock, turning to face two stunning figures. Both looked statuesque and radiated tremendous power—power that

Christopher could feel in his very soul, for these were two goddesses that could affect the soul itself.

Styx was the taller of the two; built strongly, she wore a pair of jeans and a white blouse. Her skin was as black as her river, as was her hair and her eyes. Shiny and solid and utterly terrifying,

Lethe was marble white, and like Styx, she was one solid color. She was leaner, willowy, and held a lazy smile on her face. She was dressed in a sundress and looked lovely and deceptively sweet.

Both boys bowed low, only to have the goddesses laugh. Styx, whose voice was a lovely tenor, shook her head. "Please, stand. You are an ambassador to us all… and you are the said ambassador's young warrior. There is no need to bow."

The boys lifted their heads, and Christopher barely saw the maternal air in their expressions. Styx, the dominant one stepped forward. "There is a reason you have been sent here. Persephone and Hades and Hela wanted you to see the most sacred of rivers, and your fate should you fall. Dante, if you break your oath, you will be torn asunder by my magic, your soul seared into nonexistence." She sighed, her eyes sorrowful.

Lethe took her own step forward. "If one or both of you perish, you will one day drink from my river and leave this realm as new beings. Fresh and new, without any memories of whom you once were. This is known to all in your world, but a reminder is something you need if you are to take fully the weight of your choices."

Christopher nodded. "I have already died before. I am all too aware of consequences."

There was a moment of silence in which Dante squeezed his hand, then stepped ahead. "I could feel Styx's magic in my soul. I am aware of what is to be…"

"Good," Hecate said as she appeared in a swirl of shadow. The boys both turned to her. "Meeting Lethe is perhaps the greatest thing that could have happened for now... until we are to meet with the Seas, which may take years as the souls of the Underworld are led to clean up the bodies of freshwater. You boys will be alone on earth to fulfill Gaia's request. I cannot help you beyond that of a typical goddess. Your task is not tied to my role as ambassador, and so you are on your own. Hera just declared as much fifteen minutes ago... The b#tch."

Everyone shuddered, but none more so than Dante. "There are monsters galore in the Freelands! Lycaon's children, the Maenads, Mania, Empousai and so many more!"

Hecate nodded, her eyes stoic and sharp. "There are more than that. Lost gods, ancient spells and memories from the war, mortal creatures altered by the Radiant energy from the previous war, and Ragnarok! There are new cursed beings and old ones. Arachne's brood, for example, and so many others... No, you must journey from town to town, safely nestled in enchanted walls."

Christopher nodded, standing tall. "I will keep him safe, my lady!"

Hecate nodded, eyes wide. "And yourself, my sweet grandson, your life holds meaning too."

"I know, but I swore to protect Dante, so his life has to come first."

Christopher could see Dante's eyes flinch at that reminder, but he knew it was true. The ambassador was saving the world, his life was just more important. Dante knew it too, no matter how much it ached in his soul.

Every single god sighed before Hades stepped closer. "That may be true, but that will not excuse you treating your life as unimportant. You were granted a second chance at life, you won't get a third chance. Mystically speaking, I mean. Treasure your time, dear boy."

"He is right," Hecate said, holding her hands out. "Now, I will be returning you both to the temple in New Olympus. Say your goodbyes. Prepare yourselves. You leave in three days. Oh, and your hound, Mr. Ghost, he will age far faster with my blessing. By the time you leave, he should be big enough to be of service in a fight, but I would still keep him out of one. Now go with our blessing, my sweet, powerful children."

Shadows rushed them, like smoke and ash, wrapping around both mortals and sending them back upwards to their temple and the realm of Gaia's majesty.

Dante loved teleporting; it was fun, faster, and magical. Proof of the divinities he lived with really. He could not wait to get good enough for that sort of magic, which might not be for years, but sooner or later it would happen.

As they appeared in the temple, right in the main hall, Dante grabbed Christopher's arm. "Let's get you some armor and weapons from Naveh. Same for myself. We need to be as prepared as possible if we are to serve Gaia and Hecate in this manner."

Christopher nodded, eyes sharp. "I need a better blade, something to fight the monsters of the Freelands, and so many others... I refuse to let you perish for a dull blade."

Dante watched as his boyfriend and warrior moved ahead, his chest tightening at the mere notion of them fighting monsters. But the sad truth was that, even without the war, it was likely, especially if they were to serve Gaia.

I cannot stop this. I have to distract myself, lest I go mad. Dante shook his head. "Let's also talk to Naveh about getting supplies for a shrine to Gaia. It should help get some order from the Nymphs and her other children."

Armed and Ready

Naveh chuckled as he presented Christopher with a blade, three feet in length and made of a mix of steel and sacred silver. It resonated through the air with a hum of power that anyone with sensitivity could feel. "This is some of my best work, do not lose it."

Christopher nodded, grabbing it in his hand. "I cannot read these runes, what do they mean?" he asked, running a hand down the sacred runes painted in blood along the blade.

"Ahh, protection, power, and the might of the soul. It channels magic very, very well and should help you fight powerful beings without drawing on magic. Stab it into the ground to create a potent barrier, but be warned it will not last forever. It is tied to a time and danger limit, six to twelve hours tops, depending on what is attacking it."

Christopher beamed. "You honor me. Thank you!"

Naveh waved aside his thanks. "I did as my goddess asked me to... and I like you. I rather you not die."

"You're a good man, Naveh."

"Yeah, yeah..." The forge master turned to Dante, who was smiling peacefully while petting their now much larger dog Mr. Ghost, and handed him a bow from his shelf. "This is a new bow, forged from Rowan and blood. It is powerful magic; Rowan cannot abide the touch of evil magic. It works by pure intent. It is the most powerful Earth magic born from living materials. Use it well. I have a hundred arrows, all tied and enchanted to your quiver, that will appear as you need them so you do not run out."

Dante grabbed the bow, shivering from its power. "Wow... thank you."

"It's my job, get over it... Now remember, be safe boys... and do not do anything stupid."

They nodded, bowing low to him, making Naveh's throat dry out. His heart ached at the notion of two mere children being forced into the Freelands, but he pushed the feeling aside. The gods gave their orders. Gaia's order specifically could never be denied; she was all-powerful and utterly ruthless when angered. Even by god standards.

Smiling, Naveh turned and faced Lenore, who was also in his office. "And you, what are you giving them?"

She rolled her eyes. "This." She waved her hand, and in a rush of blue smoke appeared a bag and two hoodies. "The bag is for Dante, it contains magical herbs, potions, and so on so you can heal properly. The hoodies are enchanted to keep you warm or cool as needed, as well as protected from harm. They are basically armor, just light and comfy!" She waved her hand again, summoning an orange collar with spikes. "This is for Mr. Ghost, it will make you able to find him always and cast protective magics should he get hurt."

The boys each put on their hoodies. Green and black for Christopher; grey and purple for Dante. Naveh watched as Christopher placed the collar on the wriggly Mr. Ghost, feeling the powerful magic settle onto the strong familiar.

"You two are so great," Dante said as he pulled Lenore into a warm hug, something Christopher joined in on, as did the exuberant Mr. Ghost, kissing everyone involved with his slobbery tongue. It was warm and sweet and made Naveh wretch a little. Soon enough they stopped and Lenore leaned down.

"Be safe, my sweets, and be smart." Lenore pet Mr. Ghost as she spoke, her voice soft and pained but unendingly strong. "The world is not a safe one; ancient magics permeate the Freelands. Step carefully into the world and make yourself known. Remember to summon the artifacts and supplies we gave you to make Gaia's shrine."

"We will be good," Christopher said, his eyes twinkling.

"Be sure that you are. You represent us all here at the temple. You are the voice of Hecate herself. Do not embarrass her or yourselves."

Dante nodded solemnly. "Yes, ma'am."

Lenore sniffled, and Naveh realized she was close to tears. "It is time for you to go now... You are ready." And with that, she stood tall. "I love you, all three of you."

"We love you too," both boys said while Mr. Ghost barked with joy.

And then she clapped... A swirl of blue shadows and mist wrapped around them, vanishing them from their place to the entrance of New Olympus.

Lenore shuddered, falling into her chair. "Those babies, those little boys, are being forced into such danger... "

Naveh walked to her, putting a hand on her shoulder. "They are wiser, strong, and energetic. I am sure they can do well. Dante is a rarely skilled magic user, Christopher is a potent warrior, and Ghost has our Lady's blessing. They are smart and powerful... They ought to be safe."

Lenore nodded. "You are right, but I have this feeling, this dread in my chest... something wrong is in the air. It is not something I can divine, but still..."

"Then we will open our hearts and be ready for it..."

"Always so wise," she teased, and they shared a smile that lasted far longer than it ought to.

Sitting on the train, on the outside with Ghost on their laps, Christopher kept his head on a swivel. People stared at them as they got on their train; the blessing of magic was clear enough to make the mystical sensitive people notice. Their status as Ambassador and Warrior was well known, cast throughout the land by Hecate and Hera, so people looked on in wonder. Christopher hated it. They had the attention, but it left them at risk. Still, he focused himself and kept his eyes sharp.

"You need to breathe," Dante teased lightly.

"I will when we are secure."

"So diligent."

Christopher smiled, knowing he was appreciated and understood, no matter Dante's teasing. "Where are we going?"

Dante shivered, his eyes cold and serious. "To Jamestown first, then somewhere outside of the protective magics, to a place that needs healing and help, a place to honor both of my magical essences and connect my gods. A place to draw on healing and strength, through Gaia and the Underworld."

Christopher's eyes widened. "You can't mean it?"

"I thought about it long and hard. Violent death causes hauntings which, in addition to pollution and whatnot, is a taint Gaia does not need. I have no choice but to return..."

"But Bolivar is where you nearly died, where your foster mother perished."

"I know, but that is all the more reason to go there."

"I only hope you are right..."

"So do I... I am working on the shrine to build now, one that will help heal Gaia, draw on her children, help heal the ghosts trapped by violent death caused by the war, and so on... I do not want to go back and be reminded of my previous weakness, but I feel it is needed. It feels right."

And so Christopher nodded. "Then that is where we are going. Let us just make sure it is safe first."

"Agreed."

Different Scars

Dante did not know why he wanted to help heal his old home. He had no real attachment to it. However, he had a few theories. The loss of memory made it difficult to move on subconsciously. Maybe he really did just want to heal the place from its horrible loss. Or maybe he was just more sentimental than he realized.

He had no good memories of the place. It had been painful more often than not, mundane at the best of times. He had longed for release most days, though he said nothing to his old foster mom Rose, or anyone else. Most people had mocked his mortality and lack of uniqueness. He had no good family members and fewer friends. Life had not been kind.

So really, he had no reason to return, but here he was going to make the place a shrine to the Underworld, and to Gaia in an attempt to heal the damage, restore the effects of pollution long past, and unite the Spirits of the land. Why he was doing this was beyond him. The mere concept of going back to Bolivar was making his soul itch, and depression threaten to spike. Thankfully he had Christopher, Mr. Ghost, and his medicine to help him get through. He could only hope and pray they could get him through the tough times to come—the promise he made to one of the most epically powerful and influential deities ever.

"That is it!" he whispered, drawing Christopher's attention. "I figured out why Bolivar—why of all the places to start, I chose that damn place. Gaia said I could feel pain and pollution. Regardless of if I like it or not, I was once tied to Bolivar. My magic likely senses its damage and seeks to rectify it, which is my nature as a healer." As he said it, there was a rush of rightness in his chest, like he had unlocked something within.

Christopher nodded, serious. "That would make sense, a lot of sense actually. Besides, as much as I dislike it, it would be a good thing to make a healing marker out of one of the scars of this brutal war. Bolivar is the start of your journey and played a part in mine. It makes sense to start there."

Sharing a pleased smile, Dante settled back into his seat, petting Ghost softly as the pup laid his head on their laps. Ghost had grown massively in the last few days, and Christopher spent every available hour when he was not training himself to train him. The dog learned oddly, magically fast, and now knew several commands such as sit, stay, fetch and bite. He was, sitting up, all the way at Dante's knee, and weighed maybe forty pounds. Magic, especially goddess magic, was an impressive booster indeed.

There was a constant buzz of magic connecting Dante and Christopher to Ghost, a thin line of power binding them and their oath to the dog. It made the dog more loyal, connective, and empathetic. They knew that the dog would risk everything for them; he had no real choice, as sad as that was. It also made the dog more powerful, his bite stronger, his speed greater, his senses sharper, and his mind far more evolved. All of this would come in majorly handy as time went on.

The whole thing—Christoper as warrior and Ghost as their shared familiar—made Dante feel oddly safe. That really was the point, but still...

Dante felt safe enough to close his eyes and fall asleep, thankful for the embrace of Hypnos and Morpheus and his lack of dreams that night, only to waken hours later, just as the train was coming into the station. Nerves burned in his chest. This was it, his first foray into the real world...

Could he handle it? Did he want to do this for real?

He would find out before he could say anything about it...

"Wow, it's so small," Christopher said as they walked through Jamestown.

"It only has a population of ten thousand; it used to have more before the gods' return. It used to be laid out randomly, but due to the dangers of the Freelands, it had to be remade on a grid and encompassed in a set of walls to protect its people. They lost a lot of old buildings and farmland, but our population is so much smaller. It is kind of okay."

Nodding, Christopher strode alongside his boyfriend as they moved toward their target, an apartment complex for visiting nobles. As a Priest/Ambassador and a warrior, they were now considered nobles. So, no one questioned them as they walked through the streets and up to the apartment complex in question.

As they entered the apartment, the magic within skimming past their skin with its protective essence, they quickly set up their stuff and then plopped on their beds. Christopher turned to his partner and smiled sadly.

"I have a question... You don't have to answer but I would appreciate it if you did."

Dante frowned, turning to face him. "What do you want to know?"

"Well, you told me you were a foster kid and you lived with someone named Rose. You said you were not close to her to the point that you did not even mourn her when she died. But... I do want to know why you were a foster kid if that is okay."

Dante sighed, letting out a long broken exhale of hair. "I... Well, I am a strong person; my siblings are not. They took my father's abuse. He starved us and hit us a lot. I look just like my mother, so it was worse for me and my sister who also resembles her. My father also hated my defiance, my resistance toward his abuse. I never fell in line or liked him or cared for him.

My stepmom also hated me for some reason, and that made him hate me more. She would lie or exaggerate or just freak out for anything I did. I never did figure out why she loathed me so much." Dante's hand went to his throat, shivering lightly, as Christopher rushed off his bed and curled into Dante's chest. Dante wrapped around him, sighing lightly. "I hate being choked; he used to do that all the time... or he would smother me, anything to invoke terror. I never..." He groaned, his eyes wide and dilated. "So little air... Can't breathe."

Christopher, remembering his healing training, put his hands on Dante's chest and breathed out, linking to the Earth. He let out a long soft, note, singing high in his throat. The air shimmered with power, and he flinched as Dante's deep well of agony rushed into him alongside fuzzy images.

Christopher saw a man, strong and well-tanned with dark hair, growling at him. Strong hands wrapped around his delicate flesh, feeling of panic and suffocation, tightening of the chest, and black dots dancing upon his vision. The images faded as Dante recovered, coming back to himself. Christopher collapsed onto his chest, shivering but concerned more for his lover.

"Are you okay?"

Dante, with tears in his eyes, nodded. "Thank you. I know what you did. I felt it... It hasn't happened in about a year, but I used to get those kinds of attacks a lot, right after I left my father's home." With his strong arms, Dante pulled Christopher tight into his body. "One day, I got accused of theft. I didn't do it, but he believed that I did it. He nearly killed me. He seemed to feel bad but I turned him in. I never thought they would care. I am pure human and they never did before, but the bruises gave them no choice. No punishment was given, but he lost his parental rights. I am happy about that; it set me on a better path..."

"No child should ever fear their parents..." Christopher said. "I never feared mine. I love them... Maybe since you are a necromancer, you can meet mine mystically and they'll adopt you."

Dante made a choking sound, it was a mix of tears and laughter. " Maybe... I am sorry you lost them, Christopher. Maybe I can help you see them again. We'll ask them if they'll adopt me too."

"That would be nice. Both things."

They stayed like that for hours, laying in the presence of pain and memories of the past so strong that they had become visible.

Then, Dante shifted. "Can you tell me about your parents? I just realized you never really speak of them."

Christopher nodded. "I was closer to my mom... Her name is Esther. She was a master with the dogs we raised, but also with plants. She is Hecate's daughter, and it showed. She was masterfully magical, way stronger than I am. She could have been a great High Priestess but she was content with caring for the dogs. She was tanned like me and had long blonde hair. She was scary when she was angry, but she rarely was. I loved her... We would sing together a lot, and sometimes she would brush out the dogs and sing and the world would stand still..." He paused as he felt Dante smile into his hair.

"That sounds amazing..." Dante smiled.

"It really was."

Christopher soon found that, if he did not stop, he would speak about his mother well into the night. Never once did Dante interrupt or make him feel bad or tease him. He just listened, and together they healed the wounds of the past.

The Freelands

Dante and Christopher, side by side, with supplies placed in enchanted bags, stepped off the train and onto the once small settlement of Bolivar. The town, once small but thriving, was now a smoldering crater filled with the remains of homes and people. Dante cringed the moment his feet touched Gaia, his powerful connection to the earth, magnified through training and actually meeting the Primordial, as well as his frightening ties to the Underworld, let and forced him to feel every single death and ounce of damage done to the world here. It was a harsh buzz of agony and misery that ebbed and flowed, crashing into his soul with anger and confusion and an unending amount of lingering fear.

A look at Christopher, whose ties were not as potent, told him that he too was affected on at least some level by the rampant damage caused by the Sea gods' petty evil. Dante grabbed his lover's arm, silently willing strength into him, not mystically but out of love. And it was love... The sharing of pain the night before had changed his feelings from puppy love into something with a thousand times more depth. They shared a piece of each other's souls now, and while that could change the nature of their love in the future, now it just increased his care for the boy—his warrior.

"What happened here?" Christopher asked.

"I don't remember. One day I went to sleep, and the next I woke up in Jamestown. I cannot remember anything, not a sound, moment, or memory." Dante shrugged. "I wish I could remember any detail, but I cannot."

Christopher turned, his eyes filled with questioning. "That's odd. Your memory is too good at times. I learned that first-hand yesterday..." Then he asked a question that Dante had never considered. "Is there a chance your mind was... mystically altered?"

Dante froze, considering with some horror that his boyfriend might be right. "Maybe. I never considered... We can ask Gaia's majesty to heal my heart if that is the cause, but for now, let us go on our mission. That must take priority."

Nodding, both boys hurried off the mystically protected station and down into the crater. They both cringed at the battered buildings—signs of magical assault and ashy remains. That no one had cleaned up or buried the bodies horrified Dante and only served to increase his desire to heal the land of the atrocity, to give peace to the lingering spirits and emotions left behind.

It took about an hour to reach the crater's center. They had to climb over countless remains and buildings, but they managed it. Once they did, Dante instantly pulled out the shrine pieces. It was simple; basically, a stone altar etched with divine symbols and scenes of nature. There were saplings too, rowan saplings, blessed by Lenore's magic and blood.

Within twenty or so minutes, they built the shrine and planted the circle of nine rowan saplings. Then, to complete the magic, Dante sat down in a meditative pose and instantly reached into the essence of Gaia. Through his closed eyes, he saw the green light of the Primal Goddess' essence.

"I need a few minutes to link her power to the shrine. That will cause her essence to radiate outward like a fountain. From there, the saplings will grow and create a potent barrier to protect the shrine from defilement. Then, I will ask Gaia to accept my offering of Underworld magic to help link them together and help the spirits present to move on. I will not be able to react while channeling her power. Touching me would prove fatal to you. You have to trust that I am doing okay."

Christopher nodded. "I understand, and I will protect you from all harm."

Smiling at his partner for a moment, Dante closed his eyes and put his hands on the shrine. Unlike his typical spells, he would not rhyme, he just had to connect to Gaia's mind and hope she accepted his offering.

Gaia, mother to us all, please accept not only this offering but my thanks for your attention and call. You gave me life, as you gave us all life, and you gave me purpose in serving a greater cause. So please, connect to this shrine and allow your direct power to radiate outward and into the greater world!

There was a shifting in the ground and in his mind as great laughter filled him. *I would be honored, my sweet son!* Gaia answered.

The magic in Dante shifted, taking on Gaia's kindness, her warmth, and her utter disdain for those that dared harm her children. He gasped and arched his back as the might of a Primal Goddess charged through him like a million bolts of lightning, like all the magma in the earth seared through his tissues. He was paralyzed, held fast by immeasurably potent magics. A scream caught in his chest, agony etched onto his face. Still, he held fast onto the power with his soul and let it all flow.

And flow it did, for what felt like hours, horrible, drawn-out hours.

Eventually, slowly, it faded...

And only then did he hear Christopher's screams.

"BACK!" Christopher yelled, brandishing his blade at the horrible beasts before him. "Twelve, twelve werewolves! Why here, why now?" he asked himself, not expecting an answer.

They had come from the houses around them, emerging from shadowy spaces and cracks, just as Dante's aura exploded in depth and potency. Christopher knew they had been drawn by the magic and likely seeking a meal or wanting to kill a threat. Who knew? All he knew was they were a threat, with their slobbering black jaws and broken eyes.

Ghost, his beloved hound, growled at them warningly. The hound's head swiveled as he paced around Dante's still form, serving his purpose nobly. Christopher did the same, grateful for his silver blade and practice with said blade. He fell into his stance, channeling what he could of Gaia's might, to increase his speed and strength, but he had a fear, a knowing, that it would never be enough. Werewolves were strong, ruthless, and aggressive. They were once human, and so immune to his skill as a charmer. They combined the smarts of humans and the natural instinct of a wolf. They were incredibly dangerous for even experienced warriors, which he was not.

Shifting his grip, Christopher, lost in his fear-ridden thoughts, barely missed one wolf lunging for his hamstring. He turned and sliced through the beast's chest, killing it instantly. The beast's breath, oddly sweet, forced a thought into Christopher's mind...

They must be starving. Only those diabetic or stuck in hunger smell like that.

And then, the wolves moved as one. He slashed and dodged, but it was too much, and before he could stop, a wolf knocked him down and clamped his jaws onto the back of his neck. He screamed, and magic exploded from him, sending the beast flying, but it was too late. The wound was grievous; once again he was going to die from a wound to the throat.

At least I died with purpose, in service to someone I love. Oddly that thought was only mildly comforting...

"AHHHH!" Christopher cringed as a voice—Dante's voice—imbued with pure power, exploded in a sudden intense wave that crashed over them all. Through bleary eyes, Christopher watched as the wolves blasted away in a wave of green energy. Their whimpers of agony told of broken bones and damaged eardrums.

Strong arms lifted him and dragged him, the jostling was agony but it cleared Christopher's vision enough to see that he crossed past several tall rowan trees. Even weak with blood loss, he could feel their magnificent mystical essence. He knew he was safe, they both were; the shrine had bonded to Gaia, and the Rowan circle's natural protective magics were only that much stronger.

The moment he stopped moving, Christopher was turned, and he saw a sobbing Dante, still glowing, looking down at him. "I surrender it, all of it! Gaia, let him live... Please, let him live!"

Without pause, before Christopher could even think to argue, he felt it. The energy of the Earth sank into Christopher's flesh with an explosive force so strong that it hurts a thousand times more than the bite or his first death. Clarity came with him, alongside a woman's sigh.

And then he felt something that haunted him...

"Dante... you're giving too much!" He realized it quickly. "You're going to damage your soul again. You're giving too much!" However, it was too late as Dante, already pale, turned the color of chalk and collapsed, a smile on his face. "No! Nooo! Come back!" he cried.

And then, holding his first love, Christopher felt Dante's soul flee his mortal vessel.

Sobbing hard, he held onto Dante's body, shaking and screaming even as he felt the curse of Lycaon, the venom-filling werewolves, sear into his existence. His teeth shifted into fangs, his eyes strained in the bright daylight, and his bones ached with the desire to shift. Most of all he felt Zeus' lingering hate—the essence powering the curse.

"So much hate... hate... so..." Eyes wide, Christopher turned back to Dante. "Hate... This is a curse. It is designed to make you suffer, but you have to live... to endure it." And just like that, a desperate ploy filled his heart. Grabbing his lover's arm, he uttered a soft prayer, not to the cruel gods but to Dante himself. "Forgive me." And then, like that, he bit his lover's arm with his new fangs and shared his new curse.

"Back again." Dante sighed, drifting in the darkness of the in-between. He felt the wound to his soul, the damage from casting magics far beyond his power and skill. Just like when he stopped the monster from killing those teens, he died and ended up in this space between life and death. "Only now Hecate cannot save me." Smiling, he drifted, slightly at peace with himself.

There was nothing to be seen, just endless emptiness, like a starless, moonless sky. No color, no light, no sound, just constant nothing. He would be there until Thanatos or Hecate found him. It could be a day or a century or maybe even longer. Who knew? He sure as Hades didn't!

"This is my life now, or maybe just my existence... just endless— OW!" Sharp, hot pain shot through him like a hornet sting, only a thousand times worse. "The heck?" He turned, looking at his astral limb, and was horrified to see it bleeding and torn, with a pattern he had never seen. Teeth obviously, but not human. "Are they eating my body? But I was in the Rowan Circle...

They can't get in, and— OH SWEET HECATE!" he screamed, bending over as hot magma swam in his astral muscles.

He shook, unable to fully grasp the agony that was his current state. Then he felt a pulling, through his wounded arm, dragging him through the dark like a magnet, faster and faster until the empty shattered and he woke up, in his body, with a gasp. The first thing he saw was Christopher, bleeding and sobbing.

"It worked!" Christopher exclaimed.

Dante panted, the pain fading. "How... I was..." And then he saw it... His warrior's eyes were yellow, like a wolf's. He had fangs, and there were grey streaks through his hair. "You're a werewolf..."

Christopher nodded slowly. "And so are you. I... To save you, I had to bit you... Please forgive me."

"Why?"

Christopher sighed. "Lycaon's curse... It is made so you have to endure pain. Zeus would not want you to die easily but suffer through it for a long time. It heals you so you can do just that... I knew that Zeus' magic, even if he is dead, would be strong enough to revive you... I am so so—"

Dante pulled him and kissed him hard as he could, ignoring his own blood covering his boyfriend's face. "You saved me," he said while pulling away. "It's fine... but... what are we going to do now? Will they even accept us? Can we even enter New Olympus? I am bound by Sacred Oath to Styx and Hecate, and you to me... We have to return."

"I have no idea."

"You can come with me."

They both jumped, turning their weary, cursed bodies to face the sudden voice, a woman's voice.

Dante nearly fainted at its source. "H-how are you alive?!" he screamed at the source, angry and hurt and confused as all hell.

Christopher looked at her confused. "Who...?" He stopped, and Dante knew he was seeing what so many had seen before when Dante and said woman were around each other. The same lips, the same cheekbones, and fair skin. The same curly dark hair. "Is that... your mother?"

The woman nodded. "Yes, it's me Thea, your mother. I am so sorry, Dante..."

Dante would have said something, anything, but before he could, stress and blood loss and injury overtook him and he fell into darkness once more.

Confessions and acceptance

Dante came to a large cave, deep and broad and filled with the sleeping bodies of over two dozen wolves. For a moment he panicked, only for his memories to return. "Oh yeah, I am one of them." Sighing, he turned two figures. The first was Ghost, sweet and orange. Second, he saw a tiny wolf, grey and light brown, curled up against him. "Christopher?" he said, realizing the fur was the same color as his lover's hair.

"Yes, that's him." He turned, not jumping as to not wake his lover, and then he faced his mother. She was not as he remembered her, she seemed older and colder and much thinner. Thea had always been sort of cold though, not fond of contact or hugs or kisses, even from her children. He knew she never wanted kids, but she had loved him and his siblings fiercely, just not as openly as he would have liked. "He is a sweet boy, he refused to let us take you until we swore to Styx to not be a danger to you. We chased off the pack that attacked you. I am so sorry we were too late to save you from our fate." She sat next to them both, her eyes sad but warm all at once.

He sighed. "Mom, how—"

"How am I here now?" She knew him well enough to read him. She was usually really good at that. "Well, that's easy. As you know your father forced me out of your life. I tried to make something of myself, make a life out of the life I no longer had. I got a job, made friends, and so on. Then, when I learned you were in foster care, I did what I could to make myself the best possible parent so I could help you. However, when I came—the day I came to Bolivar to talk to the judge and make my case—the attack happened."

He frowned. "What happened? I can't remember at all."

"Sirens fell on the town. Their song lulled us all into something akin to sleep." She turned to face him and he saw her stunning light blue eyes. They were so beautiful; he envied them, always had. "If you were already sleeping, since they attacked at night, I imagine the effect was more pronounced."

"Likely, yes, and mystically yes."

She beamed. "I can smell the magic on you. I always knew you'd become a witch or a priest. You were too intelligent to be anything basic."

"What else happened?" He tried to pretend he was not moved by his mom's words, but it was difficult. She was extremely judgmental, so her words held more power.

"Well, at first nothing, just constant song... then an explosion. It knocked me into a wall, almost killing me. It was pure energy, grey and blue and filled with malice. I was badly injured, something in me broken, but the wolves came. One found me and offered me the bite, knowing its magic would heal me as it did you. I rose up the ranks and soon was acting as healer of the pack. I smelled you and I came running, but we had to face our rival pack, a bunch of scavengers that butchered most of the survivors of the pack before." She leaned in and kissed his brow. "I saved you... before."

"Huh?"

"Did you ever wonder why you survived but your foster mom did not? I found you and pulled you out of the wreckage. I pretended to be a volunteer; I got you to the train so you could be taken to Jamestown. I was not in control of my dual form yet... or I would have hurt you, killed you even, if I was angered enough. I needed you safe, not in danger."

Dante breathed, drawing on Underworld energy as much as he could safely manage, and reached out to his mother. He divined that she was telling the truth. A smile crossed his face. "Thank you."

"Anytime."

Beside him, Christopher whimpered and then stood up, shimmering until he was mortal once more. "That is a nice story, but what now?"

Thea sighed. "You must stay here... Learn to control your form so you are not a danger to others. I would contact your goddess so she knows where you are."

"That is wise." Dante leaned back. "Mother Hecate, Goddess of Magic and Crossroads, answer my plea." He drew on more power, straight from the Underworld, and filled his prayer with it.

Hecate answered immediately, her essence filling the world around him. She appeared in a swirl of shadow. "I already know, Dante, Christopher." Her tone was lacking in judgment or cruelty, but it was tight and sad. "Your mother is right, Dante, you must stay here. I cannot allow you into the city until you are fully in control. I will inform Lenore and Naveh, but you must stay here... I will not hold it against you, as my Ambassador. I am sure Gaia will not hold it against you... Speaking of, I felt your creation of her shrine. I am sure all magically aligned beings did. It was remarkable. Well done."

He smiled at his goddess. "Thank you... And I will do what I can. I am sure Christopher and I will learn to control our form swiftly. I will not allow this change to ruin my duties as an ambassador."

"I am sure you will not, but you must know that this curse is old and powerful. A strong will is not going to be enough. Not alone anyway..." She sighed. "I must depart... Be safe, my darlings... and be careful." Her form evaporated, and Dante knew that she had done all she could without breaking ancient laws.

"It's a pity she cannot save us all..." He turned to his mother. "What now? How do we gain control?"

Thea's eyes were not at all warm. "It will not be easy, but honestly, effort. You must accept your temper, deal with your trauma, and either reject or embrace the curse for all it is. Which path you choose is up to you."

Whimpering like the wolf he now was, Dante nodded, "Very well..."

He looked toward the cave entrance, watching the sunrise on not just a new day but a very new life, one he did not choose. But like becoming a witch, he was sure he would make the most of it.

Maybe...